MESHING WITH THE GARGOYLE
A PARANORMAL'S LOVE 38

BY

CHARLIE RICHARDS

DEDICATION

*Call it a clan, call it a network, call it a tribe, call it a family —
whatever you call it, whoever you are, you need one.
~Jane Howard*

CHAPTER ONE

Aaron Boltson stared, shocked into silence.

What the hell is she *doing here?*

When Aaron had opened the door to his room at the bed and breakfast where he was staying, he'd been certain it would be his brother, Aziel. Aziel was supposed to be picking him up to take him to a barbeque at the estate where he lived. He would have just driven himself, but after traveling over three hundred miles — from his home in Colorado Springs to Durango — his older model *Ford* pick-up had crapped out on him.

In truth, it hadn't come as a surprise to Aaron. He'd been nursing the transmission along for nearly three months. Aaron had been struggling to scrape enough cash together to fix it, since Melanie had a habit of going on splurging sprees.

At least the estate where Aziel lived had its own private mechanic. The mechanic — Grigoris — had picked it up with a car-hauler, and he'd taken Aaron's truck to the estate to work on it. Aziel had offered Aaron the use of his truck, but Aaron had declined. Other than to visit Aziel, he hadn't had anywhere to go.

In truth, Aaron had just wanted to stay in his room and lick his wounds, metaphorically speaking. Walking in on Melanie — his wife of twelve years — being fucked by her physical fitness instructor in the bed they shared had damn near torn his heart out. Listening to Melanie's laughter at his shocked and hurt questions, then her callous comment about how she couldn't stand to touch his fat body anymore, had finished the

1

job.

Aaron had packed a bag and left, immediately calling Aziel. His brother had insisted that he come to Durango, and he'd even booked a room with an open-ended stay at a bed and breakfast. Aaron sure had appreciated it, although he wasn't too certain about the trip to the strip club Aziel's buddy had set up the second night he was there.

That had been the prior weekend.

Two days before, Aaron had utilized the services of a lawyer who'd been the sister of a detective friend of Aziel's. He'd started the divorce process. Aaron was still trying to decide how much to fight for what were his share of things or if he just wanted to give Melanie everything to make her go away as swiftly as possible. One thing that Aaron had done was frozen their joint credit card accounts.

The idea of ending his relationship with Melanie had never entered his mind until he'd walked in on her cheating on him, and getting his mind around it was taking some time.

So what the hell is Melanie doing standing at my door . . . and how did she find me?

"Hi, Aaron," Melanie purred, offering him a sultry smile. Stepping close, she settled her hands on his chest. "I'm so sorry about the way I talked to you last week. I was just so surprised to see you."

She *was surprised?*

Aaron opened his mouth to voice that thought, but the words stuck in his throat. Feeling her hands rub over his pectorals created a weird response of pleasure and distaste. Her thumbs teased over his polo-shirt-covered nipples, causing them to bead, even as the same move made his gut twist uncomfortably.

"Won't you invite me in, handsome?" Melanie started to lift onto her toes. With the way she tipped her head, Aaron knew she was angling for a kiss. "We can curl up on the bed and talk." Melanie began lowering her left hand along his torso, gliding over the ample flesh of his stomach. "Maybe do more."

Melanie's fingers eased under his protruding belly to tease at the waistband of his jeans.

Not too long ago, Aaron knew his blood would have fired swiftly upon feeling Melanie's touch. His body responded more slowly, but it did respond. Aaron felt his prick begin to thicken in anticipation.

It *had* been a long time.

Except, then Melanie's words from the prior week echoed through his mind as he recalled the sight of her trainer's bare ass as he pumped away between his wife's spread legs.

"What did you expect, Aaron? Look at you. I can't stand touching your fat body anymore."

Any flicker of arousal died a quick death, which Aaron mentally acknowledged was for the best.

Frowning, Aaron took a step backward, separating them. Unfortunately, his retreat also left space for Melanie to enter the room. She continued to smile as she moved forward, obviously mistaking his reaction — or maybe not caring. Aaron just didn't know anymore.

When Melanie reached for his hand, Aaron shook his head and drew further away.

I really need to get my shit together and find my tongue.

Melanie paused, her black brows furrowing. She pursed her full lips into a hurt-looking mew. Her light-brown skin appeared to flush, and her brown eyes took on a gleam as if she were hurt.

At one time, Aaron would have done anything, said *anything*, to get that expression off Melanie's face.

Now, however, the memory of how she'd looked as she'd mocked him was still too fresh in his mind, seeming to superimpose itself on her even then.

"Hey." Aziel's anger-filled voice cut through the air. "What are you doing here, Melanie?"

Aaron looked over Melanie's head and spotted Aziel stalking swiftly toward them. A deep scowl marred his normally friendly features. His attention was pinned on Melanie, and if Aaron hadn't known his brother, even he would have been intimidated.

"Oh. H-Hello, Aziel," Melanie stuttered. She went for innocent as she shrugged one slender shoulder. "I'm just here patching things up with Aaron." With a soft titter, she added, "I'm sure he told you about our misunderstanding."

"It wasn't a misunderstanding," Aziel growled, entering the room through the still-open door. He stopped beside Aaron and rested his hand on his shoulder, offering support. "You cheated on my brother and said some nasty shit to him." Focusing on Aaron, Aziel looked him up and down. Whatever he saw caused a flicker of concern to cross his features. Instead of addressing whatever it was, his brother stated, "You look ready to go. Shall we?"

Then Aziel used his grip on Aaron's shoulder to urge him toward the door.

While Aziel had ended up being the taller brother by a couple of inches, Aaron didn't remember him being so strong. Still, he appreciated it because it got his feet moving. Aaron tore his attention away from Melanie and started toward the door.

"Wait a minute," Melanie called, but when she reached for Aaron, Aziel stepped between them, blocking her. Undeterred, she added, "Aaron, we have things to discuss."

"If Aaron wants to discuss anything with you, he'll call you," Aziel declared. "Until then, leave him alone."

"Aaron, don't let your brother come between us," Melanie demanded, her voice hardening and taking on a demanding quality that had caused Aaron to always acquiesce in the past. "You don't allow family to come between a husband and wife."

Scoffing, Aziel released Aaron so he could close the door behind them.

Aaron noticed his brother made certain it was locked.

Melanie took advantage, slipping around Aziel and getting into Aaron's space once more. "Come on, baby," she crooned, gripping his left arm with both hands. "Don't go. I really need to talk to you." Using a silky tone that had always turned him to putty in the past, Melanie purred, "It's super important, baby."

Absently, Aaron noticed that her nails were painted red. The last time he'd seen her, they had been a pale pink. At some point in the last week, she'd taken the time for a manicure.

"Aaron?" Aziel rumbled softly, touching his lower back. "Ready to go?"

Aaron jerked his attention to his brother. "Ready," he managed to mutter before frowning at Melanie. "You didn't even apologize."

With a shake of his head, Aaron turned toward the stairs, pulling his arm free of her grip.

"I'm sorry," Melanie whined, her voice telling Aaron that she followed as he started down the stairs. "Is that what you want to hear?"

Aaron appreciated that Aziel followed behind him, forcing more space between them. "Maybe if you meant it," he muttered practically under his breath. Aaron could hear the insincerity in her voice.

Reaching the bottom of the steps, Aaron lengthened his stride and headed toward the front door. Aziel easily kept pace. Aaron heard Melanie's heels clicking on the tile, telling him she needed to trot to keep up.

"Aaron Boltson, you stop this instant," Melanie ordered, obviously tired of feigning guilt. "You will stay and talk to me."

Ignoring Melanie caused Aaron's gut to churn and his heart to ache, but he did it. He knew he wasn't in the right headspace to discuss anything with her. In truth, Aaron feared he would give in to whatever she wanted if he faced her right then.

As Aaron exited the bed and breakfast, Aziel murmured, "I'm on the right. It's unlocked."

Aaron nodded, spotting his brother's truck. While it felt a little cowardly, he hurried to the vehicle and climbed into the passenger seat. Aaron even closed and locked his door.

A second later, the door handle thumped as Melanie tried to open it. She knocked on the window, calling his name and demanding he open the door.

After pulling on his seatbelt, Aaron twisted his fingers together in his lap and stared straight ahead, doing his best to ignore her as well as the feeling of wanting to throw up.

Aziel fired up his truck and began easing out of the parking spot. Fortunately, Melanie backed up a step, getting out of the way, before she stormed to her own vehicle.

For an instant, Aaron feared she intended to follow them in her car. His brother, perhaps sharing his concern, tore ass out of the driveway. He made several quick turns in the neighborhood, taking an alternate route to the road they needed.

Aaron occasionally glanced in the side mirror while focusing on keeping his breathing steady.

When Aziel rested his hand over Aaron's, he jolted. He turned his head and focused on his brother. He saw Aziel glance his way a couple of times, then refocus on the road. A muscle ticked in Aziel's jaw.

Finally, Aziel asked, "Are you okay?" His black brows furrowed as he continued, "If I overstepped, if you wanted to talk to her, I apologize."

"No, I'm not okay," Aaron admitted, gripping Aziel's hand

and squeezing once before releasing. As Aziel returned his hand to the wheel, Aaron murmured, "I thought it was you at the door. I wouldn't have opened it if I'd known it was her." While Aaron stared out the window, he didn't really see the trees. The memory of Melanie acting all flirty filled his mind. "She was acting as if what she did was just . . . some small misunderstanding." Unable to help how small his voice sounded, Aaron whispered, "How could she do that?" He shook his head slowly. "I don't even know how long she was having an affair." Another painful thought occurred to him. "Maybe this wasn't even the first one."

Aziel squeezed his hand again. "I'm so sorry, big bro."

"Me, too." Rubbing both hands over his face, Aaron swallowed hard. "Thank you." He focused on Aziel. "For getting me out of there."

"Anytime, Aaron." Aziel flashed a tight smile Aaron's way. "I always got your back."

Aaron forced himself to return Aziel's smile.

Watching Aziel enter a code into the security box, Aaron absently repeated the numbers to himself, needing something to focus on other than his shitty life.

Definitely not where I thought I'd be at thirty-two.

"Um, I don't know if I should offer this or not," Aziel stated as he started his truck forward again.

"Offer what?" Aaron winced. "Please don't offer to take me to another strip club."

Aziel chuckled softly, smiling at him. "Naw. Not my scene, either." Then he sobered and stated, "If you want, I can have Raymond do a deep dive into Melanie's activities over the last several years." He winced before adding, "If you really want to know if this affair was the only one or not."

Aaron opened his mouth to say no. He'd already filed for divorce, so what did it matter? Except, Melanie seemed to want to reconcile. She'd been his wife for twelve years.

Do I love her enough to try again?

Could I ever trust her again?

"Yeah," Aaron murmured, nodding slowly. "I'd appreciate that."

While Aaron realized that if this hadn't been Melanie's first affair, the knowledge would be painful, he knew he needed to know.

"Okay." Aziel parked the truck and turned to face him. "I'll talk to Raymond about it this evening." Then he patted Aaron's knee and smiled. "Try to forget all that tonight, okay? Just relax and have a good time. The food's fantastic."

Aaron nodded once more. "Right."

With the way his gut still churned uncomfortably, he didn't know how he was going to eat, but he would try.

An hour later, Aaron felt even more maudlin than when he'd arrived. He hadn't realized how many people there were couples. Aaron didn't care that, like his brother, many of them were two men.

No, instead, it was how sweet and loving they all were to each other.

With his own relationship in shambles, watching them caused his throat to close for a new reason—jealousy. He hated the feeling, but he couldn't help himself.

Aaron spotted the gardens off to the side, and he headed that way, figuring it would be a good way to get away for a bit and clear his mind.

"Everything okay?" Aziel asked, jogging over to him, worry in his tone.

Pointing, Aaron indicated the garden maze. "Just gonna take a stroll." He patted his big belly and lied, "Ate too much and want to move a little."

Even as Aziel nodded slowly, he didn't appear convinced. "Okay. See you in a bit." He tapped the phone attached to his belt as he smirked. "Call if you get lost."

Aaron forced a chuckle of his own. "Will do."

CHAPTER TWO

Winging between treetops, Grimley enjoyed the wind on his face and body. He relished a leisurely flight first thing every evening when the sun set, allowing him to rise from roost. Having lived nearly a millennium, Grimley found few things truly enjoyable anymore, but flying was still one of them.

Grimley beat his wings twice before dipping the right one, veering in that direction. The gargoyle estate was only a mile away, and he toyed with the idea of visiting. When Grimley had purchased the several hundred acres and crumbling estate, he'd had every intention of hiding away in the area forever.

Then Grimley had run across Chieftain Maelgwn when the other gargoyle had been flying through the area. They'd talked for hours, and he'd found himself impressed by the large dark-blue male. Maelgwn hadn't cared that Grimley had been cast out of his prior clutch centuries before. When he'd shared the reasons, Maelgwn had not only understood but had admitted that he would have made the same choices.

When Chieftain Maelgwn revealed that he was searching for a new territory for his small clutch, Grimley had shown him the crumbling estate. The other gargoyle had accepted his offer, and for the first time in nearly three hundred years, Grimley was once again part of a clutch. That hadn't meant he'd been interested in a leadership position or even being all that friendly.

Instead, Grimley had continued with his plans to build a

small stone cottage. He lived there, visiting the estate every few weeks for supplies. On occasion, one of the inner circle would drop by to share news.

When Grimley had given Chieftain Maelgwn the estate, he never would have anticipated the chain of events to follow. He'd watched Maelgwn's clutch grow to several dozen gargoyles. That had been followed by nearly all of them finding their mates—the other half of their souls—the one person a gargoyle could bond with, allowing them to go through molt, gain a human form, and no longer be forced into roost when the sun rose.

On occasion, Grimley had felt a hint of jealousy, but it didn't linger long. He would have to socialize to possibly find his mate. Grimley was damn reclusive and too set in his ways to change.

Oh, well.

Changing directions, Grimley decided against visiting the estate. Instead, he headed for the pond. He skimmed just over the surface. Dipping a hand in the water, he created ripples as well as a fine spray, and he hummed upon feeling the moisture seep into his black hide.

To the left, Grimley spotted an albino alligator exiting the water. When the reptile changed into a naked man, he wasn't surprised, and he took a few seconds to admire the shifter's pale, muscular form. When another male greeted him with a kiss before wrapping a towel around the shifter's shoulders, Grimley smiled.

Having shifters on the estate had been a recent change. He would occasionally sit in the upper branches of the tall pines and watch them frolic in animal form beneath him. He'd spotted horses, rhinos, and lynx. There were even boa constrictors and giant otters that enjoyed swimming in the pond with the alligator.

So much has changed.

The scents of several different types of food teased the sensitive receptors on his tongue, and his mouth watered. That was another thing that had changed. Many gargoyles had found their mates in college-aged humans. The group had really lightened everyone up. Now the estate held barbeques nearly every weekend.

Unwilling to get involved with that throng, Grimley headed deeper into the forest. He flapped his wings, rising higher in the air. The droplets of water that still clung to his hide quickly dried, and he twirled and dipped in the air.

After another half an hour, Grimley could no longer deny his growling stomach. He turned back toward his cottage, flying more slowly, relaxing in the air.

Grimley had nearly reached his home when a pleasant, masculine scent teased his senses . . . for just an instant. It was there and gone so swiftly, he could have imagined it. Except, his reaction to it told him he hadn't.

His blood heated in his veins, a jolt of lust slamming through him. His dick thickened to half-mast, and his gut twisted . . . and not from hunger.

Tipping his wings, Grimley brought himself to a stop. He beat the air, keeping himself steady, rising and falling slightly with the movement. As the sensations eased, he slowly turned in midair.

What the hell was that?

Grimley hadn't had a reaction like that in . . . he couldn't even remember. Over the centuries, sex had slowly become just another bodily function. He treated the need for release the same as if he were hungry or needed to defecate. If the urge struck him, Grimley took care of it . . . and it didn't happen very often anymore.

Hesitating, Grimley didn't know if he wanted to find the source or not. With how strongly and swiftly it had affected him, he knew having it could become an obsession. Still, Grimley was never one to allow fear to rule him.

Flying slowly back in the direction he'd come, Grimley searched for the source of the smell. He inhaled deeply as he flew. It took him a few minutes to catch the aroma again.

When Grimley did, he had to fight back a moan. His mouth watered, his teeth ached, and his erection tented his loincloth obscenely. Pressing the heel of his palm to his throbbing dick, Grimley felt the crazy urge to jack off as swiftly as possible.

What the hell?

The snap of a branch followed by a muttered curse drew Grimley's attention to the forest floor. He sank lower and lower until he spotted a hint of medium blue between the branches. The intoxicating scent also increased, and Grimley swallowed the resulting saliva.

The blue belonged to a polo shirt on a large black human.

Grimley didn't recognize the man who was slowly bush-wacking through the pine trees. He didn't recognize him as the mate of any of his fellow clutch-members. He wasn't dressed for hiking, and he was damn far away from any hiking trails in the nearby national forest.

Who is he?

Creeping along a branch, Grimley drew closer to the human. He took in the way the dark-skinned male bent awkwardly to get under a branch, cursing when it caught on the fabric of his shirt, and Grimley decided he probably wasn't much of an outdoorsman. The heavy-set human was also wearing shoes more geared toward walking down a street than hiking in the mountains. Either way, he was clearly lost.

As Grimley unclipped his phone from one of the straps that cross-crossed his chest, intending to text an alert to Chieftain Maelgwn, the mild evening breeze intensified for just a moment. The human's wonderful scent thickened, making Grimley's senses sing with need.

Oh, gods.

Realization finally hit Grimley.

This lost human is my mate.

Grimley sat in shock for so long that he lost sight of the man.

Upon hearing the man murmur, "Holy shit. This is beautiful," Grimley snapped back to attention.

Grimley tucked his wings close and hurriedly crept through the branches.

"Maybe they have a working phone," the man muttered.

Recognizing the area, Grimley realized that the man had stumbled upon his cottage. He paused on a branch at the edge of the clearing. Taking in the man's clearly impressed visage, a wealth of pride filled Grimley.

My mate likes the look of my home.

Over the centuries, Grimley had read plenty of stories. He'd fashioned his small home after an old-world cottage. It had one bedroom and a fireplace where he cooked his meals. When indoor plumbing was invented, Grimley had worked with Maelgwn to create an addition in the back for a large bathroom. He'd planted flowers around the front under the windows, and he'd created a garden in the back.

"Is anyone home?"

Upon hearing his human's call as well as his knock, Grimley wondered what to do. He glanced at his phone again, thinking he should contact his chieftain. Maelgwn would know what to do. The chieftain's mate was human, after all.

"Shit," his human hissed. He lifted a cell phone toward the sky and started walking in a circle. "Still no signal." He turned around and lifted his hand to knock again.

Not liking the acrid distress scent seeping into the human's delicious aroma, Grimley rumbled, "I'm not in the house."

The big human spun to face the forest, and Grimley got his first really good look at the man. As the guy peered around, obviously trying to spot Grimley, he swept his gaze over the gift Fate had granted him. His human was big, several inches over six feet. He'd shaved his black hair close to his scalp. His eyes were probably brown, but it was tough to tell from so far away. He had medium-brown skin that appeared smooth, and Grimley couldn't wait to see what it felt like beneath his claws. He had wide shoulders and a thick build, with a bit of an overhanging gut.

Big with plenty of padding. My mate is just perfect for fucking.
"Hello?"

Right. Focus.

"You said you needed a phone?" Grimley asked, trying to keep his deep voice soft.

"Uh, yeah." He lifted his own. "I don't have service."

"You can borrow mine," Grimley told him. Then he realized another problem. "Who are you going to call?"

"My brother. Aziel," the man told him, moving slowly in Grimley's direction. "There's an estate around here, and he lives there with his partner, Jerome." Running a palm over his head, he added, "I started walking in their garden, then wandered into the trees, and now I have no clue how to get back there." Squinting up in his direction, he asked, "You wouldn't happen to know how to get back there, would you?"

Grimley figured the human was rambling from nerves, but he didn't bother to try to stop him. He enjoyed the man's melodious tenor. He could listen to his mate's chatter all day long.

Finally realizing the man had asked a question, Grimley answered. "Yeah. I know it."

The human had come from the estate. While Grimley had never personally chatted with Aziel and Jerome, he knew *of* them.

So this is Aziel's brother. Clearly older. And he came from the estate.

Does that mean he knows about us?

Through the grapevine, Grimley had heard the rumors of how Aziel had known about the paranormal before ever arriving at the estate. The human's mother had shared the information with him when he was a kid. Their existence hadn't been a surprise to him. It only made sense that his brother would know, too.

Perfect.

Dropping from the tree, Grimley spread his wings to catch himself. He landed lightly on the ground, ten feet in front of his mate. Holding out his phone, he murmured, "Here."

Aziel's brother's eyes widened. His jaw sagged open. He stumbled backward a few steps as a squeak escaped his throat. Then he dropped in a faint.

"Shit," Grimley snarled, leaping forward.

Grimley just managed to catch the human before he cracked his head on one of the stones of the cobbled walkway. Carefully, Grimley eased his mate the rest of the way to the ground. Unable to help himself, after he'd clipped his phone back to his strap, he skimmed his black-clawed fingers over his mate's scalp. The bristly hair teased his fingers, and he smiled.

Then Grimley sobered and shook his head. His mate had fainted at the sight of him. Obviously, even if the man knew about gargoyles, he hadn't been ready for one to drop out of the tree in front of him.

Shaking his head again, Grimley slid his arms under his mate's torso and legs. He hefted his big human into his arms, rising to his feet. For a moment, he just clutched his human to his chest, getting a feel for his weight while reveling in the knowledge that he had his mate in his arms.

Never thought this day would come.

Grimley stared at his mate, admiring him. "You're completely perfect, my mate," he murmured before dipping his head and touching his nose to the man's neck. He inhaled deeply, taking in his human's heady, masculine scent. His cock throbbed behind his loincloth, and he let out a low groan of pleasure and need. Shaking his head at himself, Grimley spread his wings and flapped. "Time to get help."

Lifting into the air, Grimley held his human securely. He

flew swiftly toward the estate. Grimley heard the commotion long before the rear of the estate came into view.

Evidently, his human had been missed.

"We'll find him, Aziel," Chieftain Maelgwn was saying. "Try to relax."

"My brother's an accountant," Aziel replied, judging from the words. "He doesn't do outdoors." He sounded clearly upset. "Hell, the most outdoors he does is a trip to a jungle-themed restaurant."

What the hell is that?

"Grateman and Treatise are already looking," Maelgwn stated, indicating a pair of trackers for the clutch. "They'll find him."

A second later, Grimley cleared the trees, and the expansive back deck came into view. Chieftain Maelgwn stood on the edge with a hand on Aziel's shoulder. The human's mate — Jerome — as well as a number of other humans and gargoyles, stood around them. They were offering support with words of assurance.

"Look!" The small purple gargoyle, Sumak, spotted him first. He pointed. "It's Grimley, and I think he's carrying your brother."

The group rushed off the deck as Grimley landed on the lawn.

"Grimley," Chieftain Maelgwn called. "What happened to him? Where'd you find him?"

"He found my house," Grimley told them.

"Damn." Enforcer Sapian shook his head. "He managed to wander that far?"

"Yes."

When the enforcer reached for his mate while asking, "What happened? Why's he unconscious?" Grimley took a step back and growled in warning.

Sapian froze, his blond brows shooting up. "Damn, Grim." Frowning, he stated, "I was just gonna take him to the doc."

"He's my mate," Grimley revealed, and a number of people gasped. "He told me he was Aziel's brother, so I dropped from the tree I was in. I must have startled him because he fainted."

"Ah, shit," Aziel muttered, running a hand over his scalp in a move very reminiscent of his brother. Shaking his head, he told him, "You didn't startle Aaron. You probably scared him."

"What?" Disbelief and unease surged through Grimley. At least it caused his aching erection to ease somewhat. "Why?"

Aziel heaved a sigh and revealed, "I haven't had the chance to talk to Aaron about the paranormal, yet." With a grimace and a shrug, he told him, "I wanted to make certain he followed through on divorcing his wife first."

"Wife? He's married?" Grimley couldn't help the growl in his tone.

When Aziel nodded, Grimley sighed deeply.

Of course Fate is going to fuck with my life once more.

Not this time, damn it.

Grimley frowned at Aziel. "You said Aaron's divorcing his wife?"

Aaron. Such a strong name for my mate.

Aziel nodded. "They're separated, but she's in town trying to win him back for some reason."

"He's mine," Grimley declared, shaking his head as he tightened his hold.

"We'll explain everything to him," Chieftain Maelgwn assured, squeezing his shoulder with his human-looking hand. "Give him here." He lifted his arms, beckoning with his fingers. "Let us help you both."

Grimley had to fight his desire to just fly back to his cottage.

Instead, Grimley allowed his chieftain to take Aaron.

CHAPTER THREE

Aaron slowly roused, groaning softly upon feeling the miscellaneous stings on his forearms. His legs also ached a little, as did his feet. Even his back hurt, as if he'd been sitting in front of his laptop for too many hours without a break.

"Hey, Aaron. Welcome back, bro."

Recognizing Aziel's voice, Aaron forced his eyelids open. He blinked a few times, allowing his eyes to adjust to the dim lighting. He realized he didn't recognize the room in which he lay, although, from the nicely appointed, heavy-duty furnishings, Aaron guessed he had to be in one of the bedrooms at the estate.

Why am I waking up here? And why do I hurt?

Memories of being lost in the woods, in the dark, entered Aaron's mind. A glance at his arms told him someone had cleaned the scratches and cuts he'd acquired while stumbling about out there. Someone had also removed his shoes and spread a blanket over his lower half, but he could feel that he still wore his jeans.

"What happened?" Aaron mumbled, scowling. Except as he turned to focus on Aziel, images popped into his head. *A small clearing lit up by moonlight. A gorgeous cottage surrounded by flowers. A deep voice speaking from the dark. And then* – Aaron jackknifed into a sitting position. "Holy fuck! Monster in the woods."

"There's no monster in the woods," Aziel countered, squeezing his hand as if he were some scared child. "I promise."

Aaron scowled at Aziel. "I know what I saw. There was a black, winged ... *thing*. It had horns and claws, and it was huge!" He wasn't even certain what to call it. "It dropped from the trees and reached for me."

Aziel held Aaron's gaze. "That wasn't a monster. His name is Grimley." He winced as he added, "I'd never actually met him until this evening, but he's definitely one of the fiercer-looking gargoyles I've seen." Scoffing, Aziel smiled crookedly at him. "His horns are pretty impressive. Plus, being all black like that?" With a shrug, Aziel added, "And Grimley was trying to hand you his phone so you could call me."

"What?" Aaron was pretty sure that wasn't what had happened. "Wait a minute." Something in Aziel's explanation caught his attention. "Did you say ... gargoyle?"

Nodding, Aziel smiled. "Yeah. Gargoyle." Then he grinned. "Do you remember Mom's stories? She told you the same bedtime stories, right? About shifters and vampires and gargoyles and other paranormal beings?"

Aaron frowned even as he nodded once. "Yeah, sure, but they were just stories."

Aziel shook his head. "Not just stories. Paranormals are real, Aaron." With his free hand, he indicated the space around them. "And this is the home of a gargoyle clutch."

Pinning his brother with a narrow-eyed stare, Aaron asked, "Are you on drugs or something?"

Blowing out a breath, Aziel rolled his eyes. "No," he stated flatly once he met Aaron's gaze once more. "Never have and never will."

"Goooood." Aaron drew the word out. Easing his hand free of Aziel's, he placed both palms on the mattress and pushed. Scooting backward, he rested his back against the headboard and shifted a pillow behind him for comfort. Finally, Aaron refocused on Aziel. "Then how could you think any of Mom's stories are true?"

God, please don't let them be true.

Aaron had thought they were damn terrifying.

"You were the one who just claimed to see a monster in the woods," Aziel pointed out dryly. With a wry smirk, he leaned back in his chair and crossed his arms over his chest. "How come *I* have to be on drugs to claim that Mom's stories were true, but I just have to take *your* word on faith about a monster?"

After opening his mouth, Aaron snapped it shut just as quickly. "Because I'm the big brother," he came up with.

Okay, that was stupid.

Snorting, Aziel shook his head. "That's stupid."

Aaron huffed a sigh. "Yeah, I thought the exact same thing as soon as I said it." He rubbed his temple, trying to ease the headache he could feel coming on. "Still . . . how can you . . ." Letting his voice fade off, Aaron didn't know how to finish as he thought of the monster in the woods.

Damn. Could gargoyles really exist? Except, what else would I call that thing?

"How can I believe Mom's stories are real?" Aziel finished Aaron's sentence for him. "For the longest time, I didn't. I just thought they were really cool stories."

"You thought they were cool?" Aaron gaped at Aziel as his brother grinned and nodded. Muttering under his breath, he admitted, "They freaked me out."

"Oh." Aziel actually looked disappointed, or maybe worried, to hear that. "Bummer," he muttered as he rubbed the back of his neck. Aziel stared at the wall for a few heartbeats, then blinked and shook his head. With a tight smile curving his lips, Aziel stated, "Well, I hope that'll change because I have so much to tell you."

Aaron wanted to tell Aziel that he didn't want to know. Except, some morbid curiosity kept him from opening his mouth. He sort of did want to know.

As if sensing Aaron's reticence, Aziel quickly added, "I'd actually planned on explaining everything because you'd need to know if you moved in here."

"Moved in here?" Confused, Aaron asked, "Why would I move in here?"

Aziel's brows furrowed. "Because I live here, and you're my brother." He hesitated a second before continuing, "And because you're divorcing your skanky, soon-to-be ex-wife, and you need a place to stay."

Aaron winced upon hearing his brother's description of Melanie. "Have you always not liked her?"

Aziel shrugged, glancing away for a few seconds before meeting his gaze again. "I guess it's not so much that I didn't like her as . . . I was angry she took you away from me." Swirling his finger in the air, he added, "I was in college here, so it wasn't as if I could move to stay close to you."

"I moved for work," Aaron murmured slowly, trying to follow Aziel's line of thinking.

Rolling his eyes, Aziel shook his head. "I'm not an idiot, Aaron," he countered. "I know you made a comfortable living with your accounting practice here in Durango, but Melanie wanted more. You could get more clients, larger clients, in a big city, which meant more money." His eyes narrowing, Aziel declared coldly, "And we both know Melanie is all about the money."

With a sigh, Aaron peered in another direction. He couldn't refute that. Living in Colorado Springs, she'd loved to go shopping, and she'd sure spent a lot of it.

Hence freezing our credit cards and shit. Huh. I wonder if that's what she wants to talk to me about.

"I didn't know you felt that way," Aaron murmured, happy to focus on something other than . . . that other stuff. "You encouraged me."

Hadn't he?

Aziel shrugged. "I didn't want to hold you back from what you wanted to do. That had been at first."

"At first?"

21

Nodding, Aziel fixed his dark-eyed gaze on him. "Then I overheard Melanie talking to one of her friends at a barbeque."

Almost afraid to ask, Aaron did anyway. "What was she saying?"

"That she finally had you convinced to move away from this Podunk town." Aziel frowned as he stared at where he folded his fingers on his lap. "She said living in a city would be so much more fun with so many more things to do. Living here was boring, and she couldn't stand it any longer."

Frowning, Aaron sighed softly. "Wow. I hadn't realized she was so unhappy. And that was before I got fat."

"What did you just say?" Aziel demanded, causing Aaron to snap his attention back to his brother. "She called you fat?"

Aaron shrugged negligently. "Sure, but it's true." He glanced pointedly at his belly, which bulged over the top of the waistband of his jeans. "Too much time in front of the computer working."

"Working to make her money to spend," Aziel grumbled. Then he brightened. "Besides, Grimley isn't going to care about that." With a scoff, he added, "Hell, being the massive gargoyle he is, he probably loves your bigger frame." Aziel smiled at Aaron, telling him, "Because gargoyles and other paranormals have increased strength"—with a roll of his eyes, he added—"as well as other things, they worry about hurting their partners." Grinning, Aziel waved his hand toward Aaron's big body. "I bet Grimley loves that you're a big guy. It'll reassure him that he won't hurt his human mate."

"What are you talking about?" Aaron wasn't following at all. "What's a mate? Why would Grimley care about what I look like? And who the hell would want a guy with a beer belly, even if I didn't get it from beer?"

While Aaron enjoyed a beer or two, his problem was the damn carbs. He loved pasta dishes and could never say no to

Italian. Aaron loved everything food . . .

Aziel cleared his throat, leveling a serious look at him. "Okay, well . . . here's the thing." After a second of hesitation, as if he were trying to gather his thoughts, he held Aaron's gaze and told him, "Paranormals live a really long time. Most of them, upward of five hundred years, and gargoyles live a ridiculously long time beyond that. In the range of a couple of millennia."

"A couple of millennia," Aaron whispered incredulously. "As in two thousand years? That millennia?" After seeing Aziel nod, Aaron couldn't help but mutter, "Damn."

Barking a laugh, Aziel grinned. "I know, right? Impressive."

"Uh, yeah." As Aaron wrapped his mind around that, he couldn't help but muse, "Imagine the things they've seen over the centuries." Aaron loved history. "The things they could tell us."

Aziel grinned. "Oh, I forgot you were a history buff." Cocking his head, he admitted, "Now, I don't know how old Grimley is, but I'd bet he'd be more than happy to share history with you." Waggling his brows, Aziel added, "While curled up in front of the fire, naked, spent from hours of love-making, he'll tell you anything you want to know."

The more Aziel had talked, the more Aaron's jaw sagged open. He'd never heard his brother talk so openly about sex. Aaron even felt his cheeks begin to heat.

Then Aziel's actual words registered, and Aaron felt as if his heart stuttered in his chest.

"A-Are you, uh, are you in-insinuating that I would a-actually do, uh, *that* with, um, Grimley?" Aaron couldn't remember the last time he'd had such a hard time saying something.

Still, Aziel seemed to understand, for he nodded even as his smile softened. "Yeah, bro." He leaned forward, resting one elbow on his thigh. "You want some water?" His eyes narrowed. "Or maybe something stronger? You look like you could use it."

"Uh, tempting," Aaron whispered. Then he shook his head. "How about just a soda? I think I'm going to need a clear head for this conversation."

"Fair enough." Aziel rose from his seat and headed toward a door. Pausing in the entrance, he turned to peer back at him. "Doc Perseus cleaned up a number of scratches from your trek through the forest. Do you need some *ibuprofen* or *aspirin* or something?"

Feeling the headache building behind his eyes, Aaron nodded. "Yeah. Thanks."

Aziel nodded back before he disappeared from the room.

Resting the back of his head against the headboard, Aaron let out a long, slow breath. He rubbed his temples with the forefingers of each hand as he thought about what his brother was telling him. Aziel actually expected him to . . . bed the gargoyle? Why would he think that?

While Aaron had never had a problem with same-sex pairings, he'd never looked at another man that way.

And why would he think I would look at a, a gargoyle *that way?*

Wait. Didn't Aziel say that I'm in some sort of gargoyle . . . den? No, that wasn't the right word. Clutch? That was it.

"Hey, you okay?"

Aaron jolted upon feeling someone's hand on his forearm. Snapping open eyelids he hadn't even realized he'd closed, he peered up at his brother. Seeing the concern in his brother's brown eyes, Aaron swallowed hard.

"N-No?"

Aaron didn't like the way his voice sort of trembled, but he couldn't help himself. His world had already been spinning out of control due to Melanie's infidelity. Now his brother was telling him about things that he'd always considered scary myths.

Aziel offered him a reassuring and understanding smile. "It'll be okay, bro. I promise." He held out a twenty-ounce bottle of orange soda — his favorite — as well as a couple of tablets. "*Aspirin*," he told him. As Aaron took the offered items, Aziel assured, "And this is a good change, Aaron. I promise it is. You'll see."

All Aaron could do was nod once before sipping the soda and swallowing the pills.

Sitting once more, a bottle of beer cradled between his palms, Aziel leaned toward him. "So, you asked about mates and looked a little shocked when I talked about having sex with a gargoyle." Obviously, Aaron's brother had picked up on more than he thought he had. "I'm not trying to freak you out, and I truly believe that finding out that Grimley is your mate is going to change your life for the better. So, I have to ask . . . have you ever been with a man or been attracted to one?"

Gaping, Aaron nearly choked on the sip of soda he'd just taken. He leaned forward and coughed, feeling the bubbles burn the back of his nose. Closing his eyes, Aaron forced a breath in through his nostrils as he felt Aziel gently rub his back.

When Aaron caught his breath, he frowned at Aziel. "You never used to talk about sex like this." He narrowed his eyes as he watched Aziel arch one black brow. "And you took me to a strip club," he grumbled. "Is this that Mitch character's influence?"

Aziel chuckled as he relaxed back in his seat. "Naw." Waggling his brows, he told him, "Guess it's just because I'm so happy and getting laid on a regular basis. I know how great it can be." Then Aziel sobered as he stared at Aaron. "And I want that for you, and I know Grimley can give it to you . . . because you're his mate." Before Aaron again asked what the hell a mate was, Aziel told him, "My lover, Jerome, is a giant otter shifter, and I'm his mate. The other half of my shifter's soul. We've bonded, and now our life-threads are entwined."

As Aaron listened to Aziel continue to explain about para-normals, bonding, life-mates, and how it would affect his life, Aaron felt his brain begin to go numb. One question kept spiraling through his mind.

This can't really be happening . . . can it?

CHAPTER FOUR

Grimley had sat outside on the balcony of the room Aaron had been placed in for hours. After Doc Perseus had checked over his mate, he had assured Grimley that the human was fine, just overwhelmed. Evidently, there was a lot more going on in Aaron's life than Grimley could even have guessed.

Aziel had stood in the doorway, leaning against the casement of one of the French doors. Glancing between Aaron and Grimley, he'd explained how Aaron was in the process of divorcing his wife, who'd been cheating on him. To make matters worse, Aziel had explained how the woman—Melanie— had shown up at Aaron's suite at the bed and breakfast, perhaps attempting a reconciliation.

Over my dead body.

When Aziel had noticed Aaron beginning to stir, he'd closed the door most of the way, using a wedge to hold it in place so the evening breeze couldn't cause it to swing.

Then Grimley had listened to Aziel and Aaron chatting, trying to explain everything. Unlike Aziel, Aaron didn't sound at all pleased by discovering the truth of their existence. Instead, the scent of Aaron's horror and disbelief, not to mention a healthy dose of fear, drifted out the open French door, teasing Grimley's nostrils and saddening him.

Grimley's shoulders slumped as he stared at his clawed hands, which rested between his knees.

My mate thinks I'm a monster. He doesn't want anything to do with me.

Feeling a hand on his shoulder, Grimley lifted his head to find Second Tobias standing beside his chair. He'd been so lost in thought that he hadn't even heard the other gargoyle fly over. Peering at the dark green gargoyle, Grimley couldn't think of a single thing to say.

To Grimley's surprise, Tobias offered him a smile that appeared . . . reassuring. The second wasn't really known for his warm and fuzzies. If gargoyles needed to talk with someone about feelings or problems, they usually went to Enforcer Sapian. Then, if needed, that gargoyle would involve the second or chieftain.

Of course, since bonding with his Iberian lynx shifter, Roland, the rumors are that he's mellowed. They must be true.

Tobias tipped his head in the direction away from the French doors. Then he stepped back and headed toward the balcony. He paused, one foot on a chair that had been pushed against it, his wings already half-spread as he peered over his shoulder at Grimley.

Understanding the silent command, Grimley rose from his chair. He strode toward the second, pausing only an instant to look over his shoulder toward the slightly open door. His need to be close to his unclaimed mate warred with obeying the clutch second.

Except, considering Grimley couldn't hold Aaron close as he wished, he figured there was no point in sticking around. He followed Tobias as the second stepped up, placing his second foot on the stone balcony. Then the green gargoyle spread his wings and leaped.

Grimley did the same, flapping twice before catching an air current. Dipping his wing, he veered to the right, following Tobias up one level and toward another wing of the estate. The other male settled on a veranda that serviced a seating area on the third story of the wing utilized by the inner circle, their mates, and their hatchlings.

Tobias led Grimley inside the estate and to the door of a

private study. The second knocked once, but he didn't wait for an answer. He opened the door and led the way inside.

Pausing in the doorway for an instant, Grimley instinctively surveyed the interior, registering who was inside. He saw Chieftain Maelgwn, Head Enforcer Einan, and Enforcer Sapian. There was also Raymond, their clutch's tech guru, as well as the small black gargoyle's human mate, Marty. All had returned to their true, gargoyle forms, and Marty held Raymond on his lap in a large, leather chair.

"Come in and shut the door, Grimley," Chieftain Maelgwn encouraged, beckoning him forward. A small, welcoming smile curved the corners of his lips as he indicated the sideboard. "Let Tobias know what you'd like, and he'll get it for you."

Grimley eased into the room before shutting the door. As he made his way to a small sofa, he glanced at the second and asked, "Bourbon, if you have it?"

"Sure do," Tobias assured, picking up a crystal decanter and a tumbler. "Congratulations, by the way." He flashed a smile at Grimley as he poured. "Finding your mate is a true blessing."

Easing onto the sofa with a huge sigh, Grimley rubbed his palms over his bare scalp. "I don't think Aaron feels that way."

"Do you know what the prevailing theory is on when Fate decides to bring mates together?" Maelgwn asked, arching one deep blue eyebrow ridge before he brought his own tumbler to his lips and took a sip.

Grimley shook his head as he accepted his drink from Tobias. "Thank you," he muttered. "In truth, I've never given it much thought." Rubbing the back of his neck, Grimley shrugged as he admitted, "I never thought I'd find my own mate. Not after—" Falling silent, he focused on his drink as he took a tentative sip.

Good brand.

"I recall you sharing some of the particulars with me, Grimley," Maelgwn rumbled softly, drawing his attention. He indicated those in the room. "They all know, and none of them hold it against you."

Jerking his attention to his chieftain, Grimley couldn't help the way his jaw sagged open. He snapped it closed a second later and growled, "They don't hold it against me that I slept with someone else's fated mate? Repeatedly?"

Raymond winced at Grimley's blunt words, while Marty's brows shot up.

Maelgwn must have caught the move, too, for he shook his head and countered, "You make it sound like you knew she was someone else's mate." Frowning at Grimley, he continued, "And we both know that's not the truth. She seduced you because she liked walking on the wild side, and let's face it" — Maelgwn waved his free hand up and down, indicating Grimley's big, black seven-foot-one-inch frame topped with spiraling six-inch horns — "you're damn intimidating. You fit the bill."

Huffing a sigh, Tobias settled into his own large chair. "She met you months before she met all the other members of your clutch, including her mate." He pinned Grimley with a hard, gray-eyed gaze. "You didn't know. Did you attempt to seduce her away from her mate once you did know?"

"Didn't have a chance," Grimley replied bluntly. "I was hauled in front of the chieftain first, since my scent was all over her."

Rolling his eyes, Sapian asked bluntly, "But would you have?"

"Of course not," Grimley admitted immediately. "That's taboo." Thinking back to that time, centuries before, he recalled the maiden who had learned of gargoyles, then found the most intimidating one to seduce — him. "I was probably only one of three in the clutch she'd met." Frowning, Grimley added, "And I wasn't the first one to have her. I just happened to be the last. The one with my scent on her."

"Did you rat out the other gargoyles that had slept with her?" Einan asked bluntly.

Grimley shook his head, scowling at the head enforcer. "Of course not." As he lifted his tumbler to his lips, he muttered, "What the hell would have been the point of that?"

"Exactly," Maelgwn stated, confusing Grimley. His chieftain smirked, obviously catching onto his scent. "You kept your peace, even though you were being kicked out of the clutch and named rogue, and it might have helped you."

Scoffing, Grimley shook his head. "Naw. That chieftain was an asshole. All that would have meant was we both would have been kicked out."

"And that's why we know you're a good gargoyle," Maelgwn told him, smiling. "And why Fate has blessed you." As Grimley thought on those words, his chieftain sipped his whiskey. Then Maelgwn grinned and told him, "And the most popular belief is that you meet your mate when either you or him need each other the most."

Sapian let out a deep breath, shaking his head. "And Aaron needs you. Trust me."

Grimley frowned as he glanced around the group. "He does?" Even as he struggled with Maelgwn's reasonings, even if they did warm his cold heart just a little, he asked, "Is this because of his wife?"

Grimley cringed just saying those words. The fact that his mate was wed to another—had been for years—caused a surge of jealous rage to simmer within him. He flexed the claws of his free hand, the desire to shred the woman who'd had the privilege of touching his human rushing through him.

Is this how Claritan felt when he discovered my scent on his mate? No wonder he wanted me gone.

After nearly four centuries, Grimley realized he could actually sympathize with the gargoyle.

Damn.

"Take a few slow deep breaths," Maelgwn encouraged, holding his gaze steadily. "Your mate is safe within the estate with his brother. There's no way his soon-to-be *ex* will get to him here."

Even as Grimley did as he'd been bidden, taking a few deep breaths, a thought pushed into his brain, and he let his next breath out on a growl. "But Aaron doesn't live here."

"We're working on fixing that," Sapian assured with a smile. "And you need to relax a bit before we continue, Grim. We don't want to have to tackle you to keep you from flying off half-cocked."

Grimley glanced around the group, finally scenting the concern that emanated from just about all of them. "What's going on?"

Maelgwn cradled his tumbler between his palms as he leaned forward. "His ex-wife has a slew of credit card debt that Aaron doesn't know anything about," his chieftain told him. "According to records, she has a separate checking account that Aaron puts money into every week. She burns through it fast, too, and there are deposits from other men's accounts as well as the occasional cash deposit."

"Cash deposits?" Grimley murmured, frowning. He could guess that the deposits from other men were from conquests she had on the line, but what about the cash? "What do you think they're from?"

"I don't want to be the one to tell him this," Raymond muttered, ducking his head. As Marty rubbed up and down his gargoyle's back, clearly intent on soothing him, the small gargoyle continued, "But I have camera footage of her selling really expensive pieces of jewelry to pawn brokers and jewelry stores." With a sigh, Raymond added, "I'm sure you can take a guess as to where Melanie is getting them."

"Either gifts from suitors, or she's stealing them," Grimley mused.

"Stealing them?" Raymond perked up at that. "I hadn't considered that." Reaching for his tablet, he muttered to himself, "I wonder if . . ."

His words died off as he began tapping away on his device, clearly deep in thought.

"Why would you guess theft?" Maelgwn asked curiously.

Grimley blew out a breath as he rubbed his thumb-claw over the cold crystal in his hand. "Well, she's obviously addicted to buying anything she wants, which means she needs a source of money other than what Aaron is giving her. To that end, she's turned to whoring herself to fund her lifestyle."

Bitch. Will this break my mate's heart even further? No matter. I'll find a way to help him through it . . . if he gives me a chance.

No. Not if. When. When he gives me a chance.

Pushing those thoughts to the side, Grimley continued to voice his train of thought. "Aziel told me Aaron walked in on Melanie being fucked in their bed. He doesn't know of her other . . . betrayals." Turning his attention on Raymond, Grimley continued, "I imagine that's why Aziel asked you to look into her?"

Raymond didn't answer.

Marty did. "Yeah, when he first arrived at the barbeque earlier this evening." Scoffing softly, the human stared lovingly at his clearly distracted mate. "Ray can never resist a puzzle, so after eating, he hurried to his office and got to work."

Pausing, Raymond pinned a heated gaze on Marty. "That's not the *only* thing we did in the office."

"No, it wasn't," Marty rumbled huskily as he eyed the gargoyle, heat flaring in his blue eyes.

As Sapian chuckled, Einan smirked. Maelgwn smiled as he shook his head. Even the corners of Tobias's lips quirked up a little.

Grimley did his best to squelch the niggle of jealousy he felt growing within him. Instead, he continued, "If she's using her body to pay for her extravagant lifestyle, then she's had many, *many* side-pieces." Narrowing his eyes, he added, "Or she's been the side-piece to many." Shaking his head, Grimley shrugged. "Which would give her access to another married man's home, so she could have chosen to steal expensive jewelry to pawn."

If Melanie was willing to step out on his sweet mate — *I know he is sweet, even after our extremely brief conversation* — than anything was possible.

"If he didn't even know if she'd had more than one affair, this is going to gut him." Grimley grimaced. Peering around the group, he swallowed hard. "He loved his wife. Didn't he?"

With a sigh, Maelgwn nodded. "From what I've gathered while talking to Aziel about him, yes. Aaron loved her." Then he quickly added, "Keep in mind, that's *loved*. Past tense. Sure, moving on is hard, but just the fact that he's here, he's already started the divorce process, is telling enough."

"What's that?" Grimley asked, confused as to what Maelgwn might be trying to say.

Maelgwn held Grimley's gaze. "Aaron accepts the truth, and he's trying to move on."

Grimley nodded. "That doesn't mean he's willing to move on with me."

"Oh, it might take a week or two." Mitch walked into the room without even knocking. He was followed — albeit far more tentatively — by his gargoyle mate, Kardamon, as well as several others. Mitch paused and rested his fists on his hips. "But he'll come around."

"Mitch," Maelgwn greeted, his tone sardonic as opposed

34

to holding censure. "To what do we owe this unexpected in-terruption?"

Mitch grinned broadly. "I heard you were talking to Grim, here." He waved toward Grimley. "And Aziel mentioned that he'd never heard of Aaron doing anything with a guy, alt-hough he is planning to ask his brother to confirm." With a confident smile, Mitch claimed, "I can give you help from the human perspective, since until Kard, I'd never considered do-ing anything with a guy." Then Mitch waggled his brows and gave Grimley a lecherous look. "Now, let's talk about these dreams Fate makes us have and how to use them to your ad-vantage."

To Grimley's surprise, Chieftain Maelgwn chuckled and offered Mitch a drink.

CHAPTER FIVE

Hearing the knocking on the door of his suite at the bed and breakfast, Aaron was afraid to check the peephole. He remained on the sofa, his feet up on the cushion beside him, and stared vacantly at the TV as he heard the knock come again. Aaron didn't know who he was more worried it would be—Melanie or Aziel.

Aaron had done his best to listen and understand all of Aziel's explanations two nights before. His brother had explained between truth and myth for the most common paranormal species—gargoyle, shifter, and vampire. Most of the information had been on the first two, since there weren't any vampires in the clutch. Not to mention, Grimley was a gargoyle, and Jerome was a shifter. His brother had wanted Aaron to understand everything about the two species.

Because Aziel is already bonded with a giant otter shifter, and he expects me to bond with that freaking huge gargoyle.

That huge gargoyle that actually carried my over three-hundred-pound ass.

Holy shit!

For some reason, Aaron found himself stuck on that fact. Aziel had told him that Grimley had flown him back to the estate after he'd, well, fainted.

Talk about something to take away my man-card.

Except, even now, after processing—sort of—everything that Aziel had shared, Aaron wasn't entirely certain he still wouldn't faint if he ran across Grimley again.

No matter what happened in my dream last night.

Aaron felt his cheeks heat when he recalled the vivid dream he'd experienced—enjoyed—in the wee hours of the morning. He'd been walking along a path beside the cottage, beautiful flowers on either side. The gargoyle had dropped from the sky behind him and wrapped his arms around Aaron.

Instead of shying away from Grimley's touch, Aaron had relaxed into it. He'd allowed the beast to take his weight, which he'd had no trouble doing. The much larger male had held Aaron steady as he nuzzled and kissed his neck, and Aaron had tipped his head to the side, offering more room. Grimley had rubbed his hand down his side, massaging and caressing his skin, not seeming to care about his ample love handle in the slightest. Then Grimley had slid his claws into the waist of his jeans, angling toward his cock, which had quickly stiffened to hard and aching. Aaron had moaned in anticipation, having missed being touched for so long, and Grimley didn't disappoint. The big male had wrapped his fingers around Aaron's length and—

The knocking on the door yanked Aaron out of his memories, and a shudder went through him. Just as he had been when he'd woken, he was hard and throbbing behind his lounging shorts. Aaron panted softly as he peered toward the door.

"Aaron, I know you're in there," Melanie called, sounding angry. "Open the door. We need to talk."

Aaron's erection died a quick death.

Huh. Since when does Melanie's voice, even upset, cause me to wilt?

It was definitely a first . . . and very telling.

Grimacing, Aaron weighed his options. He could tell her to leave him alone through the door, but he didn't think she would listen. After living with the woman for twelve years, Aaron knew she always expected to get her way.

In truth, he was partly to blame for that. In the early years, he'd loved pleasing her and had always tried his best to satisfy her every whim. Too bad that, over the years, those whims became way too hard to please, and he just hadn't been able to keep up with them.

Maybe that's why she stepped out on the marriage. I couldn't keep her satisfied. Maybe if I—

No! Stop, damn it! Her cheating is not my fault.

Blowing out a breath, Aaron picked up his phone. No way did he want to face Melanie by himself. He texted a quick message to Aziel—even though he'd ignored his brother's last three calls—hoping he would respond swiftly.

Melanie is at my door. Says she needs to talk to me about something. I don't want to face her alone.

To Aaron's utter relief, Aziel's response came almost immediately.

Collin is at the precinct in town. He'll be at your room in five minutes. Stall her until then. Me and a few others are on our way.

Okay. After responding with the one word, Aaron grimaced and quickly added, *Thanks.*

Aaron uncurled from his position on the sofa as his phone chimed again. He pulled up the text.

You're my brother. I'm always here for you.

Aaron smiled, until he heard Melanie call, "I heard your phone go off, Aaron Boltson. Open the door right this instant!"

After letting out a deep sigh, Aaron called, "Give me a couple of minutes to get dressed." Then he started toward where his suitcase was resting on a stand near the closet. While he'd unpacked half of his things—nice shirts and slacks that would wrinkle—most of his other things were still in there.

"You don't have to get dressed on my account." Melanie's silkily purred words almost didn't make it through the door.

Instead of arousing Aaron, even though that tone always had in the past, Aaron barely resisted rolling his eyes. He couldn't believe how Melanie was coming onto him like a bitch-cat in heat. He couldn't remember the last time that had happened.

Wait. When was the last time she came onto me . . . at all?

Aaron truly couldn't remember, which just made him sad. Shaking his head, he shucked his shorts, folded them in half, and placed them off to the side. He grabbed a pair of white briefs and yanked them on. Then Aaron pulled on the pair of jeans he'd worn the evening before to visit the nearby local diner for dinner — *Goldy's Burgers and Bites*. Their double bacon cheeseburger had been absolutely fantastic.

Taking his time, Aaron did his best to ignore Melanie's continued knocking. He just grunted a, "Hang on," each time and continued dressing. Aaron chose a button-down green shirt before sliding his bare feet into his *Dockers*.

"Well, here goes nothin'," Aaron muttered, hoping he'd taken long enough to where Collin would be there soon. The detective had always been nice, and he hoped the man didn't mind being pulled away from whatever he'd been doing while on the job . . . at least, not too much. "I'll have to buy him and his partner a beer to make up for it."

At that thought, Aaron froze halfway to the door. He couldn't shake the question of whether or not Collin was a paranormal. Maybe his partner was?

Shit. Are there even indicators that would tell me?

Hearing Melanie's insistent knock once more, Aaron pushed the thoughts out of his mind. He didn't know if Aziel had told him, or if he had, Aaron didn't remember. He wasn't even certain he wanted to know, anyway.

God, as if my world isn't upside down already.

Just that fast, another idea popped into his brain, startling him with its oddness.

If Melanie turned my world upside down, does that mean Grimley can right it?

Shaking his head, Aaron finished his walk to the door. He unlocked the deadbolt and knob slowly, placing his foot a few inches from the base. That way, when he opened it, Melanie wouldn't be able to push her way inside . . . something Aaron felt certain she would try to do.

Aaron took a fortifying breath before turning the knob and opening it just a few inches before it was stopped by his foot. "Hello, Melanie," he rumbled, meeting her gaze. "After hearing your last words at the house we shared, I don't think we have anything to discuss."

He couldn't help but notice that Melanie looked put together as always. She sported a pale-blue pants suit with matching spike heels. Her toes were painted a blue that matched almost perfectly. Even Melanie's satchel was damn-near the same hue.

Except, for some reason, Aaron thought she looked completely out of place. The smile on her maroon-painted lips and the sparkle in her brown eyes seemed even odder. She peered at him from beneath her mascara-thickened lashes while fluttering said lashes at him.

"There you are, baby," Melanie cooed. "It's so nice to see you." Her lips turning into a pout, she added, "Your brother isn't going to interrupt us this time, is he?" Putting a hand on the door, Melanie pushed, and a surprised light entered her eyes when she met resistance. "We need to talk, and I'd really like privacy."

As pleading as the expression on Melanie's face was, Aaron couldn't drum up enough interest to feel a need to fulfill her wish. He suddenly felt as if he was seeing her through a set of glasses . . . glasses that showed him her true intent. Aaron could suddenly see underneath her words and manners to the manipulation beneath.

Aaron felt something break loose inside him. He felt a wash of coldness. With his foot holding the door mostly closed, Aaron wrapped his arms around himself, wishing he had on a jacket.

"Baby?" Melanie reached through the several-inch gap and touched his arm. "Open the door, baby."

The touch was cold and caused the hairs on his arm to stand on end. He barely resisted jerking away from her. Instead, he rubbed over his arm, dislodging her fingers as he swiveled his hips, removing the unwanted touch.

"You demand a lot," Aaron muttered, scowling at Melanie. "How come I never noticed before?"

"What?" Melanie reared back as if struck. Her features first appeared shocked, followed by annoyed. She quickly cleared that expression in order to appear a strange mixture of confusion and upset. "I don't understand why you'd say something like that," she pouted, acting as if she were hurt. "That's so mean."

"Mean?" Aaron couldn't help himself as he barked a laugh. "Seriously? *Mean?*" He saw the flash of annoyance in her brown eyes before she could hide it behind her mask of unhappiness. For the first time in his life, Aaron didn't care, even if she was truly upset. He realized he could no longer actually tell. "Look. We really don't have anything to discuss, Melanie. I don't know why you came here, and frankly, I don't care." Before Melanie could reply, Aaron told her, "I know you were served with the divorce papers yesterday. Please just sign them, and we'll both get on with our lives." Unable to help himself, he muttered, "You've obviously been getting on with your life for quite some time."

When Melanie reared back as if Aaron had smacked her, he thought he should maybe feel some vindication or satisfaction. Except, he didn't. He didn't feel anything except tired. Perhaps that was because Aaron didn't feel confident that Melanie actually felt upset.

God, is everything about her fake?

Aaron just couldn't tell anymore.

"A-Aaron," Melanie squeaked. "I-I can't b-believe you'd say something l-like that." She blinked quickly, as if fighting back tears.

"What would you like me to say, Melanie?" Aaron replied, suddenly feeling tired. "How long were you cheating on me?" He couldn't help the words coming out of his mouth, even though he feared the answers . . . even if she would tell him the truth . . . which he didn't feel confident in. *Isn't that sad?* "Was he even the first one? Or just another in a long line of men to please you because your husband is too fat and disgusting to touch?"

"How dare you," Melanie hissed, her veneer of sultry femme fatale slipping. Then she seemed to catch herself, and she sniffled, touching the base of her nose with a forefinger. "This is Aziel's influence, isn't it? He never liked me."

Aaron barely resisted rolling his eyes.

Fortunately, Collin's voice called to him before Aaron had to figure out a response. "Hey, Aaron," the detective called. "You ready to head to lunch?" Then, as if he'd turned from where he'd topped the steps and had just noticed her, Collin dipped his head in a silent hello to her before refocusing on Aaron. "Or are you discussing the divorce proceedings with Melanie? Need me to sit in?"

After a grateful glance toward Collin, Aaron focused on Melanie. He couldn't help but notice a slight reddening of her cheeks, even beneath her make-up and light mocha skin. Even her brown eyes glimmered with banked anger, probably due to the fact that they were being interrupted.

"Did you want to discuss the divorce proceedings, Melanie?" Aaron asked bluntly, feeling a measure of relief, helping him to relax at no longer being alone. He didn't know why he felt so disturbed with being alone with Melanie, but he did. "We can sit there in the sitting area." Aaron pointed to the left, where the bed and breakfast had set up a large sitting area with a kitchenette. "I can make you a cup of coffee, and we can talk about how to split our assets."

Maybe she wants the house, but how she'd manage to buy it out is a mystery.

Melanie hadn't bothered to hold down a job since two months prior to their marriage.

"We are not getting a divorce, Aaron," Melanie insisted. Her voice sounded strained in a way that he didn't recognize even as he saw her feign upset by placing the back of her free hand against her forehead. "I didn't want to tell you like this, but you haven't given me any choice." There was a definite whine in her voice. There were even tears glistening in her eyes as she stared at him with a pleading expression. "Honey, I'm pregnant." Her smile appeared tremulous. "You're gonna be a father."

Gaping, Aaron felt gobsmacked as he stared at her.

A father?

In truth, Aaron had wanted to be a father for years, but Melanie had always put him off. She hadn't wanted to give up their — her — freedom, or their — her — lifestyle. For Melanie to spring this on him now . . . after getting filed with divorce papers . . . disbelief began to fill him fast and hard.

Clearing his throat, Aaron noticed the way Collin's brows furrowed. The man also had his phone in one hand and appeared to be sending a discreet text. He returned his focus to Melanie.

Aaron took in the slight flash in Melanie's eyes, something that had always indicated pleasure in the past, as if she knew she was about to get her way.

The hairs instantly stood on end on Aaron's neck.

Without thinking, Aaron asked, "Is it even mine?"

With a gasp, Melanie hauled back her arm and swung.

The crack of his wife's palm against Aaron's cheek registered before the pain . . . and he stood frozen as Collin grabbed her and forced her hands behind her back.

"Aaron? You okay, Aaron?"

Aaron realized that had to have been the second or maybe the third time the detective had asked him that. Snapping back to focus on him, Aaron answered honestly, "I-I don't know."

CHAPTER SIX

Grimley hadn't bothered with an evening flight after waking from roost. Instead, he'd made himself a cup of tea and drank it on the back stone patio after starting a fire in the metal fire pit. Relaxing in a large hammock-chair, Grimley used one leg to swing slowly as he drank his tea.

He hadn't even made it through the entire cup when he heard the flap of wings.

Barely resisting the urge to growl, Grimley wondered which well-meaning gargoyle was dropping by to offer congratulations and words of encouragement. Never in the hundred-plus years of sharing the property with the clutch had so many people visited. A few of his clutch-mates would be hard-pressed to even find his home.

Except, it seemed that Grimley finding his mate had made the rounds swiftly, and suddenly, other gargoyle seemed to think that meant he was personable and friendly . . . or that he needed advice.

In truth, Grimley did need advice. He could accept that. That didn't mean he wanted it from every Tom, Dick, and Harry in the clutch.

"Grimley?"

Upon hearing Chieftain Maelgwn's call, Grimley arched one eyebrow ridge. He couldn't imagine why his chieftain would be there. The gargoyle could have just called him.

On the tail of that realization blossomed another.

Something must have happened.

"Round back," Grimley called, stopping his momentum

and straightening in his hammock chair.

Before he'd managed to rise, Maelgwn appeared. His chieftain spotted him and waved a hand. "No need to get up." He glanced around the space, his attention lingering on the night-blooming flowers, glowing tiki torches, and fire in the raised metal pit. "I don't think I've ever been back here before." Then Maelgwn squinted as he cocked his head. "Or maybe it was right after I'd helped you build this cottage, so you hadn't created this gorgeous oasis, yet."

Grimley nodded, even as wariness permeated him. "That sounds about right." He glanced around. "I made this myself over the last few decades."

He'd wanted a place where he could relax in solitude, enjoying the simple pleasure of a safe fire. To Grimley, there was truly nothing as wonderful as the simpleness of cooking his meal over a fire. He even had a metal spit-construction that he could maneuver over his raised metal fire pit.

Nothing like the smell of a couple of fresh, plump hares roasting over an open fire.

Hmmm . . . I wonder if Aaron likes rabbit. Bet he'll like my rabbit.

Grimley's mouth began to water just at the thought of food while a sense of satisfaction filled him upon thinking of providing for his handsome human.

"Something happened today."

Hearing the seriousness in his chieftain's tone yanked Grimley from his pleasant musings. He snapped his attention to Maelgwn, seeing that he'd settled on a nearby stone fence that separated his patio from his garden on the right side of the cottage. The male leaned toward the fire and appeared to be warming his palms.

"What happened?" Grimley asked softly, seeing the tight set of the other gargoyle's shoulders.

Maelgwn lifted his head and met Grimley's gaze with a serious one of his own. "Your mate's ex-wife came by Aaron's suite at the bed and breakfast again," he revealed, causing Grimley to growl. To his relief, Maelgwn ignored him in favor of telling him, "Aaron must not have wanted to see her alone, so he reached out to Aziel. Aziel texted Detective Collin DeSoto. Collin hurried over there to offer Aaron support." Rubbing the back of his neck, Maelgwn glanced from Grimley to the fire and back again. Then his chieftain stated, "She's claiming to be pregnant with Aaron's babe."

Grimley opened his mouth, then snapped it shut just as quickly. Frowning, he stared into his tea, his brain churning wildly. He had a feeling his mate was a man of honor. Did that mean he would want to return to his wife to help with the child?

As selfish as the thought was, Grimley couldn't help but wonder where that would leave him.

Finally, Grimley lifted his attention to his silent, patiently waiting chieftain. "Is it his?"

Grimley would never attempt to come between a father and his child, no matter what Fate decreed.

"I don't know," Maelgwn admitted with a shake of his head. "I wasn't there to scent her, and Collin isn't a paranormal, so it's not as if he could say, either, although his cop instincts are screaming that it's just another manipulation."

Nodding slowly, Grimley murmured, "With the number of partners she's been with, there's the chances that a condom or birth control failed . . . assuming she used one every time." Talking about his mate and copulation with his wife left a bad taste in his mouth, and he had to take a swig of his tea to swallow back the bile threatening to rise. "How can we tell? Are there tests?"

Grimley knew that modern medicine had come a long way, but he hadn't really kept up on it. He didn't know when a parental test could be done, only that it could. If Aaron wouldn't know until after the baby was born if it was his own,

Grimley wondered just how long it would be before he would have a chance to woo his mate . . . assuming he would ever get a chance.

"There are tests that can be done immediately, if Melanie will submit to them," Maelgwn told him. His chieftain probably saw his confusion, for he added, "Human doctors can tell a lot about an unborn babe even in the womb, but it's the mother's choice to have those tests done." Growling softly, Maelgwn added, "And with the way it seems the bitch is trying to trap Aaron into staying with her, well, I don't see her agreeing."

After finishing his tea, Grimley focused on his chieftain. "Is there anything we can do?"

"Of course." To Grimley's surprise, Maelgwn smiled widely. "I've already contacted Master Adalric in Sante Fe. He's sending one of his trackers to us. Callahan Wistern."

Grimley nodded absently, knowing that his chieftain was friends with Vampire Master Adalric Bachmeier. Hell, the vampire had met his beloved—a vampire's term for mate—while at Maelgwn's clutch. While Grimley had heard that Maelgwn considered them square for his aid in helping save his mate, Bobby, he doubted the vampire saw it that way.

And that'll work in my favor.

"So, Master Adalric is sending Callahan to trance Melanie," Grimley guessed, referring to a vampire's ability to mentally manipulate a human into doing as they wished. "And he'll have her undergo the needed tests."

Maelgwn smirked. "It's even easier than that, actually." Waggling his eyebrow ridges, he told him, "Due to a vampire's need to drink blood to survive, they have the ability to discern many things from just the scent of it."

"What do you mean?" Grimley hadn't spent a whole lot of time with vampires over the centuries, and he couldn't remember specifics about all their abilities. "What can they do?"

Grinning, Maelgwn explained, "While not every vampire

has such a refined palate for the scent of blood, the average vampire can tell not only the person's blood type, but if they've recently used chemicals, which will taint their blood. In a woman, they can discern the increase of hCG in their blood." Evidently, Grimley's blank look told Maelgwn that he didn't understand, for his chieftain explained, "That's human chorionic gonadotropin."

Grimley nodded slowly, even though that still didn't mean much to him. "Okay."

Maelgwn chuckled softly. "Anyway, what the more discerning vampires can tell, is the blood of the growing babe within a pregnant woman," he told him. "If the babe is a blood type that could not have come from Aaron, then he'll give us a heads up immediately." Shrugging, Maelgwn added, "Trancing and waiting on hospital tests will be a second resort."

"Oh, damn." Grimley scoffed in wonder. "That's an impressive ability."

"Agreed."

Grimley pulled his mind away from those thoughts as he thought of Aaron. "How did Aaron take it?"

Maelgwn sobered quickly. "He's struggling, which is understandable." Peering into the fire, he told him, "Aziel shared that Aaron has always wanted to be a father, so I bet the prospect of a babe is exciting to him."

"If it's his, does Aziel think Aaron will stay with his wife?" Grimley asked the question that nearly caused bile to rise up his throat.

To Grimley's surprise, Maelgwn growled as he rose to his feet. His chieftain stalked toward him, causing him to stiffen. When the head gargoyle smacked him on the back of his head just hard enough to sting but not enough to knock him from his hammock, Grimley gaped up at him.

"What?" he mumbled inanely, rubbing his head.

Maelgwn rolled his eyes. "Nearly a thousand years old and you still worry like a hatchling." Even as Grimley stiffened in anger, his chieftain crossed his arms and scowled down at him. "Fate revealed your mate to you. He needs you. You would really sit back and let him go back to an abusive, controlling wife?"

Put that way . . .

"No," Grimley growled, shaking his head. "No, I wouldn't." With a huff, he declared, "I'll always want what's best for my mate, and that's not it."

"Good," Maelgwn stated gruffly. "Because what's best for your mate, is the one being on this earth who'll put Aaron's needs, best interests, and happiness above his own."

Grimley nodded slowly, agreeing silently, before he paused and looked up at his chieftain questioningly.

Maelgwn rolled his eyes. "That's you, dumbass."

After grumbling under his breath for a few seconds, Grimley told his chieftain, "You've been spending too much time with college kids."

Barking a laugh, Maelgwn nodded once. "You could be right." Then he sobered as he focused on Grimley. "Aziel brought Aaron here for supper."

Grimley sucked in a sharp breath, and he immediately began extricating himself from the hammock chair.

My mate is so close.

Even as Grimley stood, Maelgwn gripped his upper arm. "Remember, he's in a delicate state right now." He squeezed lightly. "He's having a meal in Aziel's suite with Jerome. Knock on the balcony door. Jerome and Aziel will be expecting it." Grimacing, Maelgwn offered, "I don't really recommend entering the suite. At least, not at first. Talk from the shadows first." His chieftain shrugged as he revealed, "It worked for me."

"Worked for you?" Grimley repeated, realizing he hadn't heard much about how Maelgwn had wooed his mate, Bobby.

Maelgwn nodded. "Are you going to put this out before you leave?" He indicated the fire.

Grimley almost started to agree, but then he paused. He recalled how much Aaron had appreciated not only his gardens, but also the look of his cottage. Considering fires were supposed to be romantic, he wondered if he could capitalize on that.

"No." Seeing his chieftain's lifted brows, Grimley knew he'd surprised his chieftain. "I'll bank it, but I won't put it out." With a swallow, he told him, "Maybe I'll get lucky and have the chance to bring Aaron out here to relax in a quiet setting."

Smiling, Maelgwn murmured, "Good idea."

To that end, Grimley moved his fire pit to the center of his stone patio. He grabbed a tall metal lattice with several hinges and positioned it around the side that faced the gardens. Then he shifted the burning timber and coals, spreading them out and making certain the fire was safe to leave.

Grimley eyed his work, knowing it would burn itself out within an hour if he didn't tend it. The way everything was situated, any sparks would either get caught on the metal fence or land on the stone patio. He nodded with satisfaction and turned his attention to Maelgwn, seeing his chieftain's smile of appreciation.

"You protect our forest."

"Always," Grimley confirmed. "This is our home."

"Indeed it is." After clapping Grimley on his shoulder lightly, Maelgwn released him and turned toward the side of the house. "Ready to go?"

"Definitely."

Spreading his wings, Grimley followed Maelgwn into the sky and toward the clutch's estate home.

A few minutes later, Grimley spotted the glow of lights illuminating the area in the distance. Nerves fired within him.

His gut bounced with butterflies even as anticipation filled him.

My mate is in there.

"Grimley."

Turning his attention to Maelgwn, Grimley couldn't find his voice.

Maelgwn smiled. "You'll do fine," he assured. "Remember, he's feeling the pull, too."

"He thinks I'm a monster," Grimley blurted out.

"That's a knee-jerk reaction that humans have all the time. He'll move past it."

Grimley had heard and scented Aaron's fear, and he wasn't so certain.

Evidently, Maelgwn picked up on his disbelief, and he chuckled. "Remember, Fate's an insistent bitch." Waggling his eyebrow ridges, he teased, "It's only been forty-eight hours, but I bet he's had a dream already."

Doing his best to keep his expression neutral, Grimley simply nodded. There was no way in hell that he would admit that he'd dreamed of Aaron already, too. He'd enjoyed every second of it, had woken up hard as nails, and within two strokes, he'd sprayed all over himself.

Gods, it'd been perfect.

Can't wait to do it with him in real life.

"Okay, I know what you're thinking about." Maelgwn shoved lightly at Grimley's upper arm, making him rock a little in the air. "I wish you all the luck, my friend." When Grimley snapped his attention to his chieftain, the gargoyle in question scoffed. "While I don't see you a whole lot, yes, I consider you my friend."

"Why?" The word was out of Grimley's mouth before he could think better of it.

Maelgwn sighed deeply even as his smile grew wide. "This." He swept his gaze around the area, indicating . . . everything. "All this, is because of you. You know that, right?"

Grimley shook his head. "No. It's because of you. You're an amazing chieftain."

"Thank you." Maelgwn smirked for a few wingbeats before sobering. "But without you, I never would have had this place. It's a sanctuary I could never have found on my own." Before Grimley could reply, Maelgwn added, "You gave this place to me, and I'll forever be grateful. Now. I need you to remember something else."

Barely swallowing around the lump in his throat upon hearing his chieftain's heartfelt words, Grimley managed to mutter, "What's that?"

As they flew, Maelgwn stated, "Grimley, you are not alone." He used a hand to once again indicate the estate. "There are so many gargoyles, and others here, who would be more than happy to help you. Remember that."

They'd reached the edge of the trees and pulled up, hovering amidst the treetops.

Grimley focused on Maelgwn, surprised to not only scent the sincerity in his tone but the earnest set of his features. It took him a second to find his voice. Finally, Grimley swallowed hard enough to get some moisture into his throat.

"Meeting you . . . it was . . ." Grimley began slowly, holding his chieftain's gaze, searching hard for the right words. "It was a gift I cannot explain. I'm the one who feels grateful." He touched his chest in emphasis. "Without you, your understanding and compassion, I would have been alone for all these centuries." Scoffing, Grimley added, "Hell, I probably would have lost the land, since I avoid anything to do with, well, anyone." Then his gaze strayed to the estate. "And I damn sure never would have met Aaron."

Chuckling, Maelgwn nodded once. "Then we both agree, Fate has blessed us both, as well as dozens of others." He sobered and reminded him, "Now, go talk to your mate, but don't forget that you have support from many, many people."

After processing that for a couple of wingbeats, Grimley nodded once more. "Thank you, Chieftain."

"You're welcome, Grimley."

Then Grimley watched Maelgwn adjust the angle of his wings and flap. In the next instant, his chieftain flew toward the left. Grimley watched patiently, letting his mind spin, as he watched Maelgwn land on a balcony in the distance. Once the male had slipped through the French doors, Grimley blinked and turned his attention to the right.

Inhaling deeply, Grimley gathered what courage he could before he rotated his wings and flapped. The move shot him toward the estate. He counted floors and balconies, locating that of Aziel and Jerome.

Someone had left the French doors ajar.

Grimley landed lightly, then paused, listening. He made out the unmistakable murmurings of voices, and a shiver worked through him. Lust slammed into him hard, and Grimley ruthlessly pushed it down, knowing it wasn't the time nor place.

Peering into the room, Grimley took in the empty, dark bedroom. He normally wasn't one to enter a person's bedroom without permission, but he figured the open French door spoke for itself. Grimley inhaled deeply before letting it out slowly . . . then he slipped inside Jerome and Aziel's suite.

Grabbing an ottoman, Grimley moved it to a dark corner of the room. He sat, listened, and breathed. For a few seconds, he just relished the earthy, musky scent of Aaron coming from the other room through the open door across the way.

"Do you really think it could be mine?"

"I don't know, Aaron," Aziel replied softly. "I suppose once we know how far along she is, you'll be able to guess, huh?"

"Right." Aaron scoffed, his voice hard. "Not like I've fucked her recently."

Even as Grimley reveled in hearing those words, he hated the harshness of Aaron's tone. Needing to speak up, Grimley rumbled, "Yours or not, we'll get through this." The image of a little babe with his mate's features filled his mind, and he murmured, "Raise it together. Our babe."

Hearing the silence fall in the other room, Grimley winced. *Shit. Why did I say it like that?*

CHAPTER SEVEN

Upon hearing the deep voice that had haunted his dreams, Aaron couldn't help the soft gasp that escaped him. He swallowed hard as his throat suddenly became dry. Grabbing his beer, Aaron took a quick swig, trying to get a little moisture into his mouth.

"Grimley? I'm assuming that's you?" Aziel called softly, and Aaron didn't miss the way he was eyeing him with concern.

"It is," Grimley confirmed, his deep voice soft and low. "Someone, uh, left the door open, so . . ." His voice trailed off, clearly uncertain.

"Yes, I left it open for you," Jerome confirmed, holding Aaron's gaze when Aaron snapped his attention to Aziel's partner. "I knew Grimley would want the chance to talk once he found out you were here." Reaching across the arms of their chairs so he could grip Aaron's forearm, Jerome told him, "Grimley can stay out of sight. I know you were worried about seeing him again." Wincing, he glanced toward the open door that led toward the bedroom. "Sorry, Grimley. I know that had to be hard to hear."

"I already know my appearance alarms Aaron." Grimley sounded resigned to that. "I hope that, in time, he'll be able to accept how I look."

Aaron knew he should say something. He just wasn't certain . . . wait. "Y-You would r-raise my child as yours?" He frowned, confused. "Why? Why would you say that?"

Grimley didn't take long to reply. "I would raise the babe

as my own because he or she is a part of you."

His soft rumbling voice caused the hairs on Aaron's arms to lift in an oddly pleasant way.

"Even if we end up having children together, I would never treat this human babe any differently," Grimley continued, sounding as if it was the most logical explanation in the world. "Well, perhaps there would be a few differences. Safety for one, since he wouldn't have paranormal strength and speed."

Aaron felt the makings of a smile tease at the corners of his lips when he realized Grimley had begun rambling. It told him the hulking male felt nervous. He found it . . . cute . . . not that he intended to ever tell him that. Most men hated to be referred to that way.

"Wait a minute," Aaron cut in, frowning as he glanced between his brother and Jerome, who were cuddled together on the sofa to his left. "Did he just say something about us having children together?" Shaking his head as he watched them exchange a look, both of them appearing surprised. "Do you mean adopting?"

"Shit," Aziel muttered, jumping to his feet. "I can't believe I forgot about that." He rushed over to where the remnants of their dinner had been left on the dining room table. "So stupid," Aziel continued as he grabbed a napkin, then placed a cinnamon roll on it. Rushing back, he held it out to Aaron. "Eat it."

Aaron stared at the cinnamon roll, which the kitchens had provided for dessert. Having eaten way too much of the delicious brick-oven baked pizza — there had been three different kinds, and all of them had been fantastic — he'd originally declined the dessert. Looking at it, Aaron still felt stuffed, and he began to shake his head, lifting a hand to ward away the offered food.

"Damn it, Aaron." Aziel thrust the food toward Aaron

again. "I need you to eat at least half of this. Then I'll explain. Okay?" Continuing to hold out the cinnamon roll, Aziel blew out a frustrated breath. "I mean it, bro. Eat it."

Rolling his eyes, Aaron set his beer on the side and took the offered treat. "What the hell is the matter with you?" he muttered, cradling the large cinnamon roll with the napkin. Aaron took a big bite. As he chewed, he glanced between the two other men. They were exchanging looks, suddenly appearing relieved. While Aaron could appreciate the sweet, cinnamony, gooey goodness, he wanted to know what the hell was going on, too. Speaking around his mouthful of food, Aaron mumbled, "So, I'm eating the damn thing. What's up?"

It wasn't until Aaron had taken another large mouthful that Aziel dropped back onto the sofa beside Jerome. He blew out a big breath and peered toward the doorway. Then he refocused on Aaron.

"So, this is gonna sound a little weird, but I swear it's true," Aziel told him as he tucked a leg under him and leaned against Jerome. It didn't seem to matter that his partner was smaller. Jerome took his weight easily, cuddling Aziel close. "And don't talk with your mouth full. It's gross."

Rolling his eyes, Aaron made a *go ahead* gesture with one hand.

Jerome nodded, opened his mouth, then shut it again.

"You guys are struggling with this, aren't you? I've been told blunt is best," Grimley commented quietly from the bedroom. Without missing a beat, he continued, "Once a gargoyle and his mate finish their bond, they have the ability to impregnate their male mate."

Aaron had just taken another bite of the cinnamon roll, and a bit of it went down the wrong way. Choking, he forced out a cough. His eyes watered, and he grabbed his beer. After managing to take a sip, Aaron frowned at Aziel, who was wincing. His brother also looked like he was about to pop up again, probably to pound Aaron on his back.

"Is Aaron okay?" Grimley asked, sounding worried.

"He's getting there," Aziel replied, still eyeing Aaron with concern. "Breathe, bro," he encouraged. "I warned you."

Finding his voice, Aaron stated gruffly, "And you also insisted I eat this damn cinnamon roll." He scowled at the pair. "What the hell?"

"Cinnamon is a natural contraceptive to gargoyle sperm," Grimley stated from the other room. "I'm glad Aziel thought about it, because I haven't eaten cinnamon in . . . a very long time." Then it sounded as if the gargoyle cleared his throat, before he quickly added, "Not that I think we're going to have sex soon or anything. I'll add it to my diet, too. Um, that way, when you're ready, there'll be no risk, and we can be free to enjoy, uh, whatever."

"You want to have sex with me?" Aaron blurted out, recalling the myriad of information Aziel had shared several evenings before when he'd been there. "Uh, to bond us." His mind reeled as he stared at the half-eaten dessert. "Even though you don't know me." Cocking his head, Aaron murmured, "It's just a biological imperative for you, isn't it? It's not like you truly care about me. How could you? You don't know me. You caught my scent, and it began a craving in you, right? That's all this is."

"Stop, Aaron." Grimley's order sounded low and rough. "Yes, I scented you, and it's created what you consider a biological imperative."

Aaron gasped, surprised at how disappointed he felt that Grimley was agreeing with him.

Which is weird because I don't actually want him, right?

"Shit, seriously, Grimley? Why would you say that?" Jerome growled under his breath as he shook his head. "Humans get so stuck on the fact that we scent them, recognize them as our mate, and want them."

"He was just being honest," Aaron murmured, feeling a

sudden need to defend the disembodied voice. "I appreciate honesty, especially now."

"You're my mate, Aaron. I'll always be honest with you," Grimley declared softly. Then he continued, "But sex isn't the only thing I want from you."

Cocking his head, Aaron couldn't help but ask, "What do you mean?"

"I mean, being mates is far more than just sex." Grimley chuckled, the noise sounding rough, as if he didn't do it nearly often enough. "I've been alone a long time. Centuries. I want to learn everything about you," Grimley claimed. "I want you to be my partner. We'll comfort each other, care for each other, and someday, I hope we'll love each other."

Aaron rubbed his chest with his free hand, his mind spinning faster the more he heard Grimley say. His heart felt as if it ached in his chest. He thought he'd had that once, but she'd betrayed him. The fact that the offer was coming from a being who was obviously male wasn't even a blip on his radar. No, instead, Aaron didn't know if he could open himself up to another.

"I know it will take time. Trust takes time, and you've been hurt." Grimley seemed to have a direct line to Aaron's thoughts. "I ache with the need to hold you, to soothe you, but I fear you're not ready for me to do that yet. Soon, I hope, though." His voice softening, Grimley murmured, "We have time, my mate. Although I want everything with you, everything as soon as possible, I can wait."

Uncertain how to respond, Aaron stared at his cinnamon roll. He took a bite, hoping for a moment to buy himself some time. Glancing between Aziel and Jerome, he tried to figure out what to say.

Aziel cleared his throat, shifting restlessly on the sofa beside Jerome for a few seconds. Then he licked his lips and murmured, "So, on our way back here, Jerome talked to Raymond." After a glance at his partner, Aziel refocused on Aaron. "I wasn't certain if I should tell you this, but seeing as you made that comment about wanting the truth, I have some tough ones to share."

Aaron swallowed the food in his mouth, the taste no longer quite so yummy. Setting aside the rest, he drained the last of his beer. Then he set that aside too and placed his palms on his thighs.

"Okay," Aaron began, rubbing his legs. Recalling that Raymond was this place's tech expert, he grimaced. "This is about Melanie, right?" He saw Aziel begin to nod and added, "You were going to have Raymond look into whether or not this was Melanie's first affair." After taking a deep breath, Aaron took a guess. "It wasn't, was it?"

Aziel winced as he shook his head. "Um, not even close," he whispered, rubbing the back of his neck in discomfort. "She . . . she—" His brother paused and grimaced, looking to Jerome as if for support or aid. Aziel's partner gave him a troubled smile, and Aziel refocused on Aaron. "Raymond found a checking account in just Melanie's name. She siphons off several hundred dollars a week into it from your joint account."

"Several hundred a week," Aaron murmured, thinking about his bank statements. Shaking his head, he stated, "No, she pays several hundred a week to a woman who runs a charity organization."

"Afraid not, Aaron," Aziel countered. "That woman with the fake organization is really her. She spends it on, well, anything she wants." After another glance at Jerome, Aziel told him, "She gets payments from other men . . . men that she's been intimate with. Um, and Raymond has found footage of her selling expensive baubles to either jewelers or pawnbrokers. Sometimes she deposits the cash into her account, but from the transactions Raymond has found, she doesn't always."

"Expensive baubles? Are you talking like, jewelry?" Aaron repeated, trying to understand what Aziel was telling him. After his brother nodded, he asked, "Where would she get . . . oh." Realization dawned on him, and he whispered, "Gifts from other men." Aziel winced even as he nodded again. "And the cash?"

Aziel opened his mouth, then snapped it shut again.

Jerome stated in a soft voice, "Raymond has traffic camera footage of her entering many of those men's homes, then exiting hours later . . . uh, clearly rumpled."

Aaron felt as if he'd been sucker punched. His breathing sped up, and he struggled to breathe properly. "H—" His voice broke, and he had to try again. "How long?"

While it wasn't the most comprehensive question, the pair seemed to know what he was asking. "Over three years," Jerome answered softly.

"Th-Three years," Aaron whispered, his breath catching in his throat. "Three . . ." He shook his head, his mind reeling. "Three . . ."

Aaron couldn't seem to comprehend it. His wife had been seeing other men, multiple men, from the sounds of it, for over three years. He thought back on their time together, wondering what he could have missed.

Could I have done something better? Was there something I wasn't giving her that she needed? Why hadn't she said something? Why didn't she feel she could talk to me about it? We —

"Easy, hey, I'm so sorry, Aaron," Aziel crooned the words into his ear. "It'll be okay. I promise." Rubbing up and down Aaron's back, his brother obviously attempted to soothe him. "We'll help you through this. You're not alone."

Even as Aaron nodded, he didn't bother opening eyelids he couldn't remember closing. He struggled to breathe, barely keeping his tears in check. Aaron didn't fight Aziel when he urged him to bend over and pushed his head between his knees.

All the while, Aziel continued urging him to breathe . . . but it was so very hard, and he felt himself becoming light-headed.

Aaron suddenly felt himself being lifted. He barked a surprised cry, but the spots flashing in front of his vision made it impossible to see what was going on. A second later, Aaron felt himself seated once more . . . on someone's lap. Black, buttery-soft fabric wrapped around him, partially obstructing his view.

"Relax, Aaron." Grimley's soft, deep voice rumbled into Aaron's ear, his warm breath ghosting over the hairs on his neck. "Let the grief out. All will be well. Just give it time."

Shocked, realizing he sat on Grimley's lap, Aaron froze. Then the oddest sensation seemed to vibrate from the male's body. The rumbling vibrations seemed to sink into Aaron's bones, melting him, relaxing him, and offering him comfort beyond anything he had ever before experienced.

Aaron found his breathing slowing. The tension eased from his body, and he sagged against the much larger male. He found himself gripping the forearms around his waist, clinging to him, and he realized he never wanted the amazing sensations to end.

"That's the way, my mate," Grimley purred quietly into his ear. "Your family is here. I am here. You're right where you belong."

Blinking slowly, Aaron began to get his vision to come into focus. He realized that it wasn't a blanket wrapped around him. Instead, the billowing dark folds were . . . wings . . . Grimley's wings!

Aaron's breathing sped up for a new reason.

I'm in the gargoyle's arms. I'm sitting on his lap. Grimley is holding me . . . and I like it.

Within the massive creature's heavily muscled arms, sitting on his thick thighs, Aaron actually felt . . . small for the first time in . . . he couldn't remember when. It was definitely a long time.

Inhaling deeply, Aaron took in what had to be the gargoyle's natural, masculine aroma. He found it a mix of earthy and fresh, like the outdoors after a summer storm. Unable to help himself, he turned his head and breathed it in.

To Aaron's surprise, he felt his prick stir. His blood began to heat, arousal hitting him faster than he'd experienced in quite some time. He breathed slowly, trying to get his suddenly racing pulse under control.

"Oh, Aaron," Grimley whispered into his ear. "You smell so fantastic, making me burn with answering desire."

The male nuzzled the crook of Aaron's neck and shoulder, and he instinctively turned his head, offering more room. Grimley groaned softly, placing a gentle, sucking kiss to his flesh, pulling a moan from Aaron's throat.

"So perfect," Grimley rumbled. "So responsive."

A shudder rolled through Aaron's body, his suddenly hard dick jerking behind the fly of his jeans.

"Uh, guys," Jerome called over the sound of the odd vibrations Grimley was making. "Simmer down there a bit, huh? We're still talking here."

CHAPTER EIGHT

Grimley felt Aaron stiffen in his arms, and he couldn't help but cast a glare Jerome's way. The giant otter shifter lifted his hands in a silent apology. Dipping his chin in a subtle nod of acceptance, Grimley had to admit that the other man was right.

Rubbing one hand down Aaron's side soothingly, Grimley slowly eased off his trilling. "Stay relaxed, if you can, Aaron," he urged once more. "We've done nothing wrong, but Jerome is right."

Aaron didn't completely relax against him. Instead, he sucked in his breath, and if Grimley didn't miss his guess, his human was trying to suck in his gut. Grimley fought his desire to growl, hating how self-conscious his mate obviously was of his body.

I'll show him how much I love every inch of him . . . someday.

In the meantime, Grimley would offer as much affection as his human would accept.

"Um, wh-what was that noise you were making?" Aaron asked softly.

Grimley noticed that his human kept his head down. He seemed to be focusing on Grimley's wings, although he kept both his hands gripping the forearm of the arm Grimley still had around his waist, holding him steady. Grimley didn't mind because it left Aaron's neck vulnerable to his licks and kisses, and his mate tasted delicious.

"Gargoyles have the ability to do something called trilling," Grimley explained softly, beyond happy to finally

65

have his mate right where he wanted him . . . in his arms. Naked would be better—his dick twitching just at the thought—but Grimley had told Aaron that he could be patient, and he would. "Trilling is a vibrating noise we make in our chest. It creates a soothing, relaxing sensation in whoever we hold. We use it to help family, hatchlings, the occasional close friend"—after pecking another kiss to Aaron's neck, Grimley finished—"and especially, our mates."

Aaron remained quiet for a few heartbeats before he murmured, "Is that why it affects me so strongly?"

"Yes, Aaron. You are my mate." Grimley had promised to always be truthful, and he wasn't about to go back on that now. "Not only will my trilling help soothe and calm you, but so will my scent and touch." He hesitated and added, "It will also arouse you."

"Huh." Aaron left it at that. Obviously changing the subject, he said, "Thank you for helping me. I . . . I've never had a panic attack before."

"You had every reason to," Grimley decided to go with. After all, his mate had just had his world rocked . . . again. Nuzzling his nose along Aaron's nape, Grimley admitted, "It's my pleasure to hold you and soothe you, and I hope I will always be here, in a position to help you."

"Because I'm your mate?"

Grimley wasn't a big fan of the slight sadness he heard in Aaron's tone or how it eased into his scent.

With a sigh, Grimley tried to figure out a way to help his human understand. "Why is that so bad?" he asked instead, confused by his mate's response. "Why does it matter that Fate is the one that decreed we'd be perfect together? It doesn't mean that it won't take work." Shaking his head, Grimley reminded, "Every relationship takes work. All Fate does is point out the magnified connection between us, which would give us the optimum chance at forging a strong bond."

"So . . . it doesn't force you to be attracted to me?" Aaron asked tentatively.

Taking a moment to truly think about the question, Grimley worked through the best way to answer. "No," he finally decided on. "Fate does not force me to be attracted to you." After a nip to the tip of Aaron's ear, Grimley told him, "I would have been attracted to you regardless of Fate's urgings."

"Why?"

Grimley blinked, confused for a second. He almost asked, "Why what?" to try to get clarification. Then, due to the dubiousness flooding Aaron's scent, it hit him.

He wants to know why I'd be attracted to him. If I ever meet his soon-to-be ex-bitch of a wife, I'll be hard-pressed not to knock her upside the head, pregnant or not.

Huh. It's possible she's lying about that, too.

"Aaron, for paranormals, attraction is a little different," Grimley began slowly, trying to find the right words that would reassure his self-conscious human. "The scent of a person is just as important as their looks." Shaking his head, Grimley amended, "For most of us, more so. If the scent of a person turns us off, even if they're the most handsome or beautiful person in the world, we won't be interested."

"Our . . . scent?" Aaron nodded slowly, his attention straying to Aziel and Jerome, who were watching in silence. "So, if I hadn't, like, showered in a week, you wouldn't be attracted?"

Grimley couldn't help it. He barked a laugh even as he shook his head. It could have been the move or the sound, but Aaron jerked his chin up, snapping his attention to his face. Grimley watched as Aaron's eyes widened, and his human sucked in a shocked gasp.

The trickle of uncertainty, along with just a smattering of fear, teased Grimley's senses as Aaron roved his gaze over his face. Only the fact that Aaron remained semi-relaxed in his hold, and that he didn't pull away, eased Grimley's sadness.

Trying to push past the awkward moment, Grimley lowered his voice to a whisper as he told him, "If you hadn't bathed in a week, I would be even *more* attracted to you, Aaron," he told his mate honestly. "Because your skin would be saturated in your natural, masculine scent, which I find beyond intoxicating." Rubbing his palm over Aaron's side, hoping to soothe, Grimley added, "It's the opposite of what you're thinking. Humans covered in artificial and chemical scents turn us off. Another thing that will send us in the other direction is the scent given off by someone with cruel or evil intentions. Those emotions give off a certain . . . aroma . . . that is not at all pleasant."

Neither was the smell of fear or anxiety, but he kept that thought to himself.

"Oh," Aaron whispered, barely breathing out the word.

His dark eyes were round in his face, but at least he didn't look away. For a few seconds, Aaron nibbled his plump bottom lip, drawing Grimley's attention to it, and he barely resisted the urge to dip his head and nibble it between his own teeth. Grimley resisted but only because he felt certain his mate wouldn't be open to that just yet.

Someday . . . soon, I hope.

"Can I, um . . . can I . . . touch you?"

Grimley felt his eyebrow ridges shoot up for an instant upon hearing Aaron's tentative question. Squashing the urge to grin—no need to scare off his mate by showcasing all his sharp teeth—he couldn't stop the way the corners of his lips curved up. Nodding slowly, Grimley agreed, pleasure filling him.

"So different," Aaron murmured, appearing to be concentrating hard on his features. As he lifted one hand from Grimley's forearm and brought it toward his face, Aaron added, "Your arm was bumpy. I can't think of anything to compare it to." Aaron touched his fingertips to Grimley's cheek, then skimmed them along his jawline to his chin. "Face is, too. Bet it would feel fantastic rubbing on . . ." Aaron snapped his mouth shut, and the scent of embarrassment rolled off of him. "Um."

Grimley fought back his urge to chuckle, although he was really, *really* interested in what Aaron had been thinking. "Yes, my skin is bumpy like that all over."

"A-All over?" Aaron's eyes were wide, and for the briefest of seconds, he glanced down, telling Grimley exactly what he was thinking about.

"Mmmm, *all* over," Grimley confirmed huskily. Then he winked and added, "Although, not quite to the same extent in certain areas as others." Taking a chance, Grimley offered, "Would you like to go somewhere private? Somewhere you can explore . . . anywhere you want?"

Aaron opened his mouth, then closed it again. Uncertainty flooded his scent, mingled with desire with a hint of trepidation. When Aaron glanced toward Aziel as if asking his opinion, Grimley knew he needed to give his mate an out.

Squeezing Aaron's hip, Grimley offered, "Another time, perhaps. When you're more comfortable with me."

"I—" Aaron paused and furrowed his brows. He glanced toward Aziel again.

Aziel smiled at him. "Grimley is your mate, Aaron," he told him with a shrug. "There's no one you'd be safer with. He would never force you to do anything you don't want to do, and his instinct drives him to keep your happiness at the forefront of everything he does." Then Aziel bobbed his head a little as he added, "As well as your safety."

Aaron grimaced for an instant before admitting, "I'm so very tempted to accept, but I don't want you to think I'm unfaithful, like my wife."

Snorting derisively, Aziel frowned at him. "You are *nothing* like your *ex*-wife," he claimed forcefully. Then he added,

"Plus, you filed for divorce before you even met Grimley, so it's not as if he impacted your decision at all." Then Aziel smirked and waggled his eyebrows. "Does that mean you're thinking about doing—" He finished by whistling suggestively.

Rolling his eyes, Aaron relaxed, saying, "You're such a goof." As Aziel grinned, Aaron turned his attention back to Grimley. "Uh, where did you have in mind?" The scent of embarrassment increased just a little, but Aaron gamely added, "Do you have a suite here, too?"

Grimley shook his head. "I do not." Squeezing Aaron's side again, he asked, "Do you remember the cottage where we first met?" After Aaron nodded, Grimley told him, "That's my home. I'd love to show it to you properly."

Aaron grimaced as he peered out a window. "I don't think I'm ready for another night hike. I hadn't meant to do that the first time."

"No hike," Grimley promised. "Instead, a night flight."

"You can't possibly think you can . . ." Aaron's voice trailed off. "Oh," he murmured. "Guess you already did."

The scent of Aaron's embarrassment intensified, tickling Grimley's senses uncomfortably.

"I'm sorry I startled you that first night," Grimley told him, squeezing Aaron's hip once more. "You were there at the estate, and your brother is mated to a shifter. I made a bad assumption."

Aaron cleared his throat as he shook his head. "Still, can't believe I fainted."

"You're not the first, Aaron," Aziel told him with a smirk. "Andre did, too, when he first met the gargoyles."

"He did?" Aaron sounded so hopeful.

Aziel chuckled. "Yep." Rising to his feet, his brother moved toward the kitchen. "Need anything for the road?" he asked, as if it was a done deal that Aaron would leave with Grimley.

Grimley mentally crossed his fingers.

"Uh, no. I don't need anything," Aaron replied.

When his mate began sliding from his lap, Grimley lowered his wings and released him, instantly missing the contact.

Aaron stood, and Grimley followed suit.

When Grimley rose to his full seven-foot-one height, he appreciated the extra-high ceilings that Maelgwn had installed throughout the estate. Otherwise, he would have needed to cock his head to avoid catching his horns. Turning to Aaron, Grimley towered over half a foot over his mate, and his human was staring up at him while backing up a step.

Grimley slowly eased back onto the chair, hoping it would help his mate be more comfortable.

Shaking his head, Aaron mumbled, "I'm sorry. Just . . . forgot how, uh, big you are." As he eyed Grimley, he added, "Shouldn't have, though. Otherwise, how could you have held me on your lap?" Aaron glanced down at himself, his expression critical as he grumbled, "I'm not exactly a small guy."

"You're perfect just the way you are," Grimley blurted out.

Aaron eyed him askance. "Uh, yeah, right."

"As you said, I'm a big guy." Grimley reached out and gently gripped Aaron's hand with his own. Lifting Aaron's hand to his mouth, he bussed a warm kiss over his palm. "I needed a mate who could handle my size, and Fate provided." Holding Aaron's gaze, Grimley did his best to express his sincerity. "You're perfect for me, Aaron."

For several seconds, Aaron stared at him in obvious disbelief. Then a shy smile curved his full dark lips. He ducked his head, cleared his throat, and rubbed the back of his neck.

"Um, th-thank you," Aaron mumbled. Shuffling his feet, he took a step toward the door. "I, uh, guess we should go?"

Gods, my mate is so damn cute.

Grimley knew better than to say that, however. Instead, he

rose to his feet and indicated toward the bedroom. "How about we leave via the balcony? It'll be easier."

After a second of hesitation, Aaron nodded. "Okay."

Pleased with Aaron's agreement, Grimley couldn't resist slipping his arm around his human's waist. He felt his mate jolt, but he didn't pull away. Grimley squeezed Aaron's hip before guiding him through the bedroom.

A moment later, Grimley and Aaron stood near the edge of the balcony. He paused, wondering how to broach the subject of the best way to carry him. Grimley hoped Aaron wouldn't resist if he once again carried him bridal style. It was just the easiest.

"Hey, Aaron," Aziel called, following them outside, making them both turn. His brother held up a jacket. "I figure it's cold flying through the air, even on a nice night light this."

"Thanks."

Aaron took the jacket and pulled it on. It appeared a little tight on the human, and he couldn't zip it, telling Grimley that the jacket was Aziel's, who, while a couple of inches taller, had a much trimmer figure. Grimley made a mental note to have his mate bring his own jacket from the bed and breakfast.

Hell, maybe I can get him to bring all his clothes and move in here.

Grimley figured Aaron wasn't ready to move directly in with him, but that didn't mean he couldn't have him close.

Then Aziel held out a phone. "This is a burner," he told his brother. "It has service all over the estate." When Aaron took it, he added, "I already programmed a bunch of numbers into it, so if you can't get me, I'm sure you can call someone else."

While Grimley didn't like the insinuation that Aaron would need anyone other than him, he held his tongue.

Instead, after Aaron had thanked Aziel, Grimley rumbled, "Once I pick you up, feel free to wrap your arms around my neck."

Grimley decided not to ask for permission. Instead, he bent, slipped his arms around Aaron, and swung him into his arms. Then he bent his knees and leaped into the air.

Ignoring Aaron's *eep* of surprise, Grimley reveled in the heady knowledge of once again having his mate in his arms.

CHAPTER NINE

Aaron clung to Grimley for several seconds, until his curiosity got the better of him. Loosening his grip, he peered around the area. He watched in wonder as the trees zipped past him, the wind blowing pleasantly on his face. The wind also made him feel grateful for Aziel's jacket, and he did his best to tug it over his prodigious girth.

God, I need to lose weight.

Although, recalling Grimley's comments, Aaron knew the gargoyle didn't care one way or another.

I do, though. I'll be healthier and happier for it.

Considering Aziel's words regarding Grimley wanting him happy and healthy, Aaron figured the gargoyle would help him in whatever he wanted. He spotted the cottage ahead and decided to think on it another time. Aaron admired the moonlit flower garden as Grimley drifted toward the ground.

Grimley bypassed the front and winged his way around back. As the gargoyle landed on a small back patio, Aaron admired how it was surrounded by a stone wall on one side, a trellis on another, and a cobblestone path leading into the woods at the back. The patio itself had a large, hammock style, hanging chair, a small metal bistro-style table, two matching chairs, and a raised metal firepit.

Aaron thought it looked cozy. There were even coals glowing in the metal firepit. As soon as Grimley eased Aaron to his feet, he crossed to it and held out his hands to warm them.

Smiling, Grimley asked, "Would you like to enjoy the

evening out here for a while? Or I could start a fire in the fire-place inside."

Aaron glanced around the nice space. He hesitated, consid-ering. The sudden gust of wind cutting through his light shirt made up his mind for him.

"Inside, if you don't mind," Aaron replied.

Grimley nodded. "We'll sit out another night." Then he led the way to the door.

Aaron smiled faintly, but he didn't comment on the male's assumption that he would be back. In truth, if the inside was as nice as the outside, then he would enjoy spending time there. Having grown up in a town on the smaller side, Aaron hadn't been a big fan of the city, but he'd wanted his wife happy.

Ex-wife, even if she isn't agreeing just yet.

Collin had confirmed that his sister — Aaron's lawyer — had served Melanie with the papers the prior day.

One way or another, I'm no longer involved with her beyond fig-uring out how to extricate myself from her.

"You coming?" Grimley asked from inside a small kitchen. "If you changed your mind—"

"No, I didn't change my mind."

Aaron hurried through the door, closing it behind him. Glancing around the space, he realized the space before him was essentially broken into two rooms. The first was a kitch-enette with cupboards, double doors that could lead to a pan-try, and food prep space. There were no modern appliances, but he noticed a door in the floor that probably led to a root cellar.

The other half of the room consisted of a number of pillows on the floor before a low-slung coffee-style table. The large fireplace that Grimley was crossing to and easily starting a blaze in held a metal frame with a swinging arm. A large Dutch-oven-style pot hung on the hook to the right of the hearth. Aaron bet that, once food was placed within it, it could be swung into the large stone fireplace to cook.

"Wow!" Aaron thought the place held a wealth of old-style charm. "This is amazing."

"It does have running water," Grimley told him, obviously misinterpreting Aaron's aww. He pointed toward one door. "There's a bedroom through there." Indicating the second door, Grimley added, "I had a bathroom addition done a few decades ago." He smiled wryly. "Couldn't resist the allure of indoor plumbing, and there's a huge soaking tub in there."

"I look forward to checking it out," Aaron told him truthfully.

Grimley appeared so earnest, and kneeling before the freshly lit fire, he didn't seem nearly as intimidating as while standing. Perhaps it was the way the firelight danced across his mottled black skin, but Aaron found his blood heating as arousal began simmering through him. The way Grimley eyed him, with clear concern swimming within the black depths of his eyes, warmed Aaron in a way he could barely comprehend.

"Aaron?" Grimley asked tentatively, sitting back on his thighs. "Can I, uh, get you a drink?"

Aaron began to shake his head, then thought better of it. "Water would be great."

Immediately hopping to his feet, Grimley crossed to the pantry doors. He opened the one on the left, revealing a spigot coming out of the wall. When Grimley turned it on, it flowed into a large basin.

Aaron guessed that spigot backed up to the plumbing added for the bathroom edition.

Grimley quickly filled two tall glasses before turning off the water. Using his hip, he closed the door. Then he tipped his head, indicating for Aaron to join him near the fire. As Aaron approached, Grimley deftly lowered himself onto a pillow, crossing his legs Indian-style before him. Then he placed one glass on the low table. He took a sip from his own, watching Aaron approach over the rim of his glass.

Something occurred to Aaron.

Grimley is just as nervous as I am.

That knowledge settled something deep within Aaron. He chose a pillow near the offered water and carefully mirrored Grimley's pose. Although, he didn't do it with nearly as much grace. Aaron picked up his water and took a deep swallow before replacing it on the table.

Aaron rested his arms on his thighs and eyed Grimley, noticing the way the gargoyle's tail twitched as if he couldn't keep still with nerves. Reaching over, he gently placed his palm on the male's tail, stopping the movement. He'd hoped to reassure the gargoyle, so he was surprised by how he sucked in a sharp breath and stared at him with wide dark eyes.

Okaaaaaay.

Pushing forward gamely, Aaron squeezed Grimley's tail lightly as he told him, "You have a lovely home, Grimley. It's so very cozy." He'd hated the cold, austere decorations Melanie had chosen. Aaron had always felt as if he were in a show home. When Grimley didn't reply, Aaron tried again. "Um, Aziel told me how gargoyles bond with their mates, and I don't think I'm ready for that, but . . . I haven't been touched in a really long time, and Aziel said your instinct would be to please me. So, I was wondering if we could maybe do some touching or something, because—"

Realizing he was rambling, Aaron snapped his mouth closed. When Grimley still didn't respond, he forced himself to meet the gargoyle's gaze. Shock flooded him when he spotted the damn near feral desire burning within the depths of Grimley's dark eyes. He had his hands clenched in his lap, and his chest rose and fell with each unsteady breath.

For all the world, Grimley looked as if he wanted to eat him . . . in the most delicious of ways.

Holy shit!

"G-Grim?" Aaron whispered, uncertainty filling him.

Grimley blinked twice as his nostrils flared. After licking his lips, he rumbled gutturally, "Y-You're petting my tail."

Aaron froze for several seconds before peering down at his lap. Sure enough, he had pulled Grimley's tail onto his thigh and had been rhythmically petting the last six inches of it. When Aaron stopped, it twitched against the inside of his thigh, dangerously close to his groin.

"Uh, sorry?" Aaron yanked his hands away as he focused on Grimley's face once more. "I-Is that, um, not allowed?" Squinting at the gargoyle's features, Aaron wondered, "Does it hurt you?"

Scoffing softly, Grimley rumbled, "Not the kind of pain you're thinking of." He stared pointedly at his loincloth-covered groin before returning his attention to Aaron. "Not that kind of pain at all."

Aaron followed Grimley's gaze and gasped upon spotting the huge tenting of the gargoyle's black loincloth. The creature's erection, while covered, was still on blatant display. It had to be at least ten or eleven inches, and there was even a wet spot showcasing where the flared head pressed against the fabric.

"Oh."

Aaron breathed the word in shock. Before his attention, the thick member in question twitched and jerked beneath the fabric. Yanking his focus back to Grimley's face, Aaron saw that the gargoyle had closed his eyes, and he was breathing slow and deep.

"Holy shit," Aaron whispered softly. "Your tail." If a lightning bolt had struck him, he wouldn't have been more shocked. "Touching it is an aphrodisiac?"

"Yes," Grimley confirmed gruffly. He slowly opened his eyes and met Aaron's gaze. "I can't remember the last time I allowed someone to touch my tail, but I don't remember it feeling as ball-tingling as your simple petting."

Aaron gaped. "R-Really?"

"Really."

"I-I-I, uh, d-didn't mean to, um." Aaron wasn't certain what to say.

Grimley chuckled roughly. "I know, Aaron." Holding Aaron's gaze, he began sliding his tail up his thigh. "I know you had no idea that stroking my tail like that was almost as good as" — he pressed his tail against the base of Aaron's jeans-covered erection, then stroked up once, twice — "massaging my cock."

Gasping, Aaron barely managed to keep still. The friction on his dick felt so damn good. He swallowed hard, trying to find words.

"You mentioned wanting to touch, to explore," Grimley growled softly, his tone full of heat. "There is nothing that I want more." His tail paused, and the gargoyle added, "We'll play with each other's bodies, learn each other's hot spots, and spend all evening spilling cum all over each other."

Aaron gaped. Never before had anyone ever spoken so bluntly, so brazenly, to him. His blood fired in his veins, heating him even further, and his nipples beaded, poking against his polo shirt. Even his cock twitched, and he could feel precum dampening his underwear.

Grimley groaned softly, his nostrils flaring. "The aroma of your need is mouth-watering, Aaron." Bowing his head, he closed his eyes as a shudder worked through the huge male. "Please tell me yes now, or I'll need to open a window to diffuse some of the scents of our desire."

Unable to deny himself after so long making do with just his right hand, Aaron whispered, "Yes. Yes, please."

With a groan, Grimley snapped open his eyelids. If possible, his features had tightened into an even more feral expression. His dark eyes appeared to glow with some inner light, but was probably just a reflection of the fire.

"My mate," Grimley rumbled, rocking to his knees. Reaching over, he grabbed a rolled-up piece of fabric from against the wall. "Gonna make you fly, Aaron." Grimley snapped out the bundle and spread it several feet before the hearth. Then he rested on the edge and held out his hand. "Will you join me?"

Aaron glanced at the fabric, realizing it was a large skin of some kind. Dismissing it, he reached out and took Grimley's hand. With far more gentleness than Aaron expected, the hulking gargoyle helped him forward, then urged him to recline onto the hide blanket. As he relaxed on it, he found it far softer than he would have expected.

Then Grimley knelt beside his hip, leaning slightly over him. His huge black wings were spread, perhaps helping him to keep his balance. Glancing from Aaron's face to his waist and back, Grimley reached for the hem of his shirt. His expression and actions told Aaron far better than any words could that the gargoyle would stop the second Aaron asked, or he met resistance.

To encourage Grimley, Aaron lifted his arms. Even though revealing his big belly was the last thing he actually wanted to do, he knew he needed to take a leap of faith. Still, Aaron couldn't help the way he nibbled his bottom lip. Hell, it had been a long, long time since he'd gotten even partly undressed before someone other than his ex.

And I should not be thinking of her while with Grimley.

Doing his best to push memories of Melanie's sneering face from his mind, Aaron lifted his shoulders when Grimley tugged the shirt up and over his head. As soon as it was off his arms, he acted on instinct and covered his flabby belly. A soft growl drew Aaron's attention to the gargoyle's face.

While Grimley's gaze still gleamed with heat, there was something else there, too. There was a mixture of anger and . . . understanding there. After Grimley tossed Aaron's shirt toward the table, he eased forward and sprawled next to him, bracketing him between the gargoyle and fire so he was warm.

"I could look at your beautiful body all day long, Aaron," Grimley told him, propping himself up on his elbow. He reached out with one clawed hand, then seemed to hesitate. Meeting Aaron's gaze, Grimley asked, "May I touch you?"

Aaron shivered, not from cold but from the desire he still saw burning within the gargoyle's dark eyes. "As long as I get to touch you back."

Grimley growled as a wide smile curved his lips. "Nothing would please me more."

Then Grimley seemed to take Aaron at his word. He rested his clawed hand on his torso before sliding it sideways. As he moved, Grimley gently teased a claw over Aaron's right nipple.

A zing of pleasure danced across Aaron's skin, and his beaded nipple pulled even tighter. He gasped softly, and heat flooded south. Pleasure simmered through Aaron's veins, and he felt his dick flex behind his fly.

"Oh, damn," Aaron whispered, resting his hands on Grimley's shoulders. "I—"

Aaron didn't know what he planned to say, and he supposed it didn't really matter. Just then, Grimley skimmed his calloused fingers up and cradled his jaw. At the same time, he leaned even closer.

"May I kiss you, Aaron?"

For a second, Aaron froze. Surprise flooded him. "Kiss?"

Grimley nodded. "Kiss." He teased his thumb along Aaron's bottom lip, causing goose bumps to spread down his neck and over his torso. "Kiss these gorgeous, plump lips. Ravish them."

"Yes, please."

That was all it took.

Grimley leaned forward and pressed his thinner black lips against Aaron's own plump ones. He didn't ask permission. He took, slipping his tongue between his lips, prying them apart easily, before leading Aaron's appendage in a dance so sensual, his body erupted with fire . . . helped along by the gargoyle's hand as it skimmed down his neck, shoulder, ribs, everywhere.

CHAPTER TEN

Grimley couldn't get enough of Aaron's taste. His mate tasted divine, and he responded even better. Everywhere Grimley skimmed his palm, teasing and massaging, Aaron moved into his touch. His human had his arms wrapped tightly around Grimley's shoulders, and he clung even as he petted the skin of Grimley's back.

Aaron arched when Grimley teased over his hard nipples. His mate trembled each time he skimmed his nails over his ribcage. When Grimley eased his fingers under his belly roll to scrape a couple of nails along the V-groove of his hip, Aaron fed him a moan and pushed into his touch.

Touch starved.

Grimley recognized the reaction because he damn near felt the same, and he reveled in the opportunity to help ease Aaron's loneliness. *And mine, too.* He loved drawing every reaction he could out of his large, gorgeous mate.

When Aaron teased around where his wing bones jutted from his back, he fed his human a moan of his own. His human must have caught on, for he wrapped his hands around them and rubbed the few inches he could. Snapping his mouth away, Grimley broke the kiss on a roar as a hard shudder worked through his body.

Between the tail petting, the kiss, touching his mate, and finally the wing bone massage, Grimley couldn't keep his body in check. The sensations rolled over him like a tidal wave, drawing him under the spell of his human's touch. His orgasm swamped his senses, and his cock throbbed as his balls pulled tight.

Grimley tucked his face against Aaron's neck as his body jolted with wave after wave of bliss. Ecstasy sang within his veins. He shuddered and jerked, riding the high that came from his mate giving him the best damn orgasm of his life. Even his teeth ached, and he barely resisted the urge to sink them in Aaron's flesh, starting their bond.

Panting hard, Grimley tried to pull himself together. If he'd come so hard just from such little stimulation, he couldn't wait to experience everything with his human.

Gods, it just might kill me, but what a way to go.

Lifting his head, Grimley peered down at Aaron, meeting his gaze. He would have felt embarrassed if the heady scent of arousal still didn't perfume the air. His human looked completely shocked.

"D-Did you just, um, come?"

Yup. Shocked mate right there.

Grimley smiled, knowing the look probably appeared more than a little satisfied. "Oh, yeah." He sighed deeply even as he scented Aaron's disbelief. "You have no idea how powerful your touch is, my mate." Continuing to appreciate Aaron's musky, needy arousal, Grimley licked his lips as he began kissing down his chest. "Now then," he mumbled against Aaron's flesh. "Now that I'm relaxed, why don't I help you with your problem?"

While Grimley felt Aaron try to suck in his stomach as he began kissing down it, he ignored the move. He also ignored the way his mate pushed at his head, as if he was afraid of having his wonderfully squishy stomach touched. Instead, Grimley doubled his effort to express his appreciation.

Grimley kissed and sucked his way down Aaron's smattering of a treasure trail. Massaging the flesh on either side, he moaned his appreciation. "Love your softness to my hardness," he mumbled as he continued working his way down.

Nuzzling Aaron's belly with his cheek, seeing as his human had appreciated his bumpy skin so much, Grimley peered up at Aaron. He noted the way his mate nibbled his bottom lip and knew he needed to find some way to help ease his human's discomfort. To that end, Grimley eased his fingers beneath the slight overhang of his belly to tease into the waistband of his jeans.

That drew a gasp from Aaron.

Much better.

"Can I open these, Aaron?" Grimley asked huskily, his need to taste his mate deepening his voice even further. As he took a deep inhale, where he relished the delicious aroma of his human's pre-cum, he recalled how gloriously Aaron had responded to his frank words from earlier. With that thought in mind, he rumbled bluntly, "I want to suck your dick, feel the heft of you on my tongue, taste your flesh and seed on my tongue."

Groaning, Aaron bucked his hips, pressing his groin harder into Grimley's face. While he could have taken that as an answer, he didn't. He wanted the words.

"Give me permission, Aaron." Grimley lifted his head just a smidge so he could peer into Aaron's heavy-lidded gaze. "This *will* start our bond," he warned. Even though it was in the simplest of ways, his mate deserved to know. "I need the words."

"Yes," Aaron moaned, his hips bucking once more. "God, please suck me. Been so long," he whined. "Need it."

Grimley once again didn't ask twice. "My mate," he crooned as he made quick work of his new and forever lover's belt and fly. Carefully, Grimley peeled down not only Aaron's jeans but his underwear, too. As he watched, Aaron's thick erection sprang from his groin, and his mouth watered. "Oh, Aaron." Gently, Grimley wrapped his clawed hand around his mate's thick, nearly ten-inch cock. "You definitely don't disappoint." As he began a light jacking, watching Aaron begin to writhe ever-so-beautifully on the elk hide, he crooned, "Can't wait to feel this in my ass."

Aaron gasped, freezing, causing Grimley to pause, worried that he'd somehow hurt his mate by accident. Peering up, he glimpsed the surprise on his mate's features. Grimley had to take a couple of deep breaths to figure out what he'd said to put that expression there.

Then it clicked.

Grinning widely, Grimley allowed a growl to enter his voice as he resumed a slow jacking of his human's gorgeous, dark brown erection. "Oh, my mate," he crooned. "You're surprised by that, aren't you?" Leaning down, Grimley stuck out his tongue and licked over Aaron's pre-cum dampened crown. "Surprised by my desire to feel your cock sliding in and out of my ass?"

"Y-Yes," Aaron managed to gasp out roughly. "Oh, god. Please do that again."

Grimley obeyed. Dipping his head, he stuck out his tongue and swiped slowly across the head. That time, he didn't stop there. Instead, Grimley moved to lave the bundle of nerves beneath his flared head, stimulating it.

Aaron barked a cry. His fingers twisted into the fabric beneath them. Arching his body, he shook as his cock twitched and belched another bead of pre-cum.

Recognizing the signs of impending orgasm, Grimley opened his mouth and wrapped his lips around Aaron's crown. He sucked hard as he sank down, burying his nose in his mate's gloriously perfumed groin. With his human's flared head lodged in the back of his throat, Grimley swallowed.

Aaron roared, a hard shudder racking him. A second later, thick pulses of seed slammed into the back of Grimley's throat, nearly making him choke. He quickly swallowed as he eased halfway off, sucking lightly. From the continued forcefulness of his pulses, coupled with the amount of them, Grimley realized just how pent-up his mate had been.

Gods, I don't want to know when it was last that he got it on with his ex-wife, but damn, it must have been ages.

Grimley pushed the thought from his mind as he sucked and drank. Finally, after what had to have been a full minute, Aaron's body stopped bucking. The twitching of his mate's dick slowed, even though cum continued to drizzle from the slit. Petting Aaron's sides, sucking gently, Grimley eased his mate down from what had to have been a fantastic release.

Peering up Aaron's body, Grimley waited for his mate's eyelids to flutter open. He blinked slowly, obviously attempting to bring his brain back online, and Grimley felt a stab of pleasure that he had done that to his human. Finally, Aaron looked down at him, a loopy smile curving his lips.

Slowly, Grimley eased off Aaron's prick, allowing the wet, still-swollen length to flop back down onto his mate's belly. To his pleasure, his mate sucked in a breath, telling him he remained sensitive but not *too* sensitive. Grimley needed to know what to expect when he took him in hand in a few minutes.

With that in mind, Grimley pushed to his knees. The stiff stickiness of his loincloth caught his attention. Grimley reached down and carefully untied his stays before easing the fabric from his groin. He carefully swiped at himself, clearing away most of his spilled cum.

When Grimley looked up, he met Aaron's wide-eyed gaze. He also noticed the aroma of uncertainty creeping into the air. Grimley fought back a wince, recalling that Aaron had never been with a man. Seeing a guy clean up or even just have a hard-on was probably a new experience for him.

Grimley figured he probably needed to slow down, but the teasing aroma of Aaron's continued arousal made thinking with his big head difficult.

After setting aside his soiled loincloth, Grimley slowly stretched out beside his mate. He laid a tentative hand on his belly, testing the waters. If he was going to freak out after being sucked off by a guy, then lying next to a naked male with both their hard-ons out, well . . . he knew this would be the time.

"How are you feeling?" Grimley asked, rubbing lightly over his chest, enjoying the feel of Aaron's smooth skin.

Aaron remained quiet for a moment, and Grimley allowed him that time to gather himself. Considering his mate continued to lie relaxed beside him, he wasn't too worried. When Aaron rested his left hand on Grimley's right forearm, he paused in petting his human. Except, when Aaron didn't push or pull at him, he resumed his light rubbing.

"I feel like . . ." Aaron's words drifted off as he swept his gaze over Grimley's bare body. Meeting his gaze once more, his human surprised him by saying, "I feel like I'm overdressed."

Chuckling, Grimley grinned broadly. "I can fix that." He quickly shimmied down Aaron's body. As he curled his claw-tipped fingers into the waist of his mate's spread jeans, Grimley met his mate's gaze once more. "You sure you're okay lying nude with me?"

Aaron smiled. "Yeah."

Grimley nodded once, then made quick work of Aaron's remaining clothes. He eased the jeans and underwear down his legs, pausing only long enough to remove his shoes and socks. With one last tug, Grimley left his mate bare before him.

Sucking in a harsh breath, Grimley couldn't help but take a second to sweep his gaze over Aaron's gorgeous, dark-skinned frame. He saw his thick thighs and wondered what they would feel like wrapped around his waist as he plundered him. His attention snagged on Aaron's still-wet dick, half-hard against his belly, and his mouth watered anew. Spotting the muscle in his pectorals and arms, Grimley recalled how Aaron had clung so tightly, and he wanted to feel that over and over.

"G-Grimley?"

Hearing and scenting the rising notes of uncertainty, Grimley quickly set to work banishing Aaron's doubts. He crawled up his lover's body, nuzzling over his flesh as he went. When Grimley reached his head, he pressed a slow, sipping kiss to Aaron's lips before he eased to his mate's left. Resting his weight on his arm, he smiled down at him as he resumed petting his human's soft torso.

"Feel better?" Grimley asked huskily, unable to disguise how much Aaron affected him. Hell, it wasn't as though he could hide his continued hard-on.

"Yeah." Aaron reached up and used his right hand to cup Grimley's jaw. Rubbing over Grimley's flesh, he began working his way up to tease his pointed ear. "You're so different, but so . . ."

Grimley found himself struggling to process Aaron's words, as his ears were sensitive. The touch of his mate sent his senses singing, and his cock throbbed with renewed need. When Aaron skimmed his fingertips to the base of Grimley's horn, he couldn't help but groan deeply.

"Damn." Aaron pausing in his ministrations allowed Grimley to catch his words. "Another hot spot?"

Humming, Grimley nodded a smidge. "Anywhere you touch is a hot spot."

Aaron snorted, rolling his eyes, not looking nearly convinced.

"You doubt me?" Grimley rocked his hips close, allowing his erection to press against Aaron's hip. "You shouldn't." He couldn't help but do it again. The stimulation just felt too damn good. Even as Aaron gasped and snapped his attention downward, Grimley asked, "I don't think you believed me when I told you that I couldn't wait to feel your erection buried deep in my ass." As he spoke, he reached down and gently took hold of Aaron's dick, pleased to find it hard once more. "Want me to prove you wrong?"

Moaning, Aaron muttered, "C-Can't believe I-I'm still hard."

"Been too long for both of us, I expect," Grimley muttered, but he didn't really want to dwell on it. Instead, as he began jacking Aaron's prick, he admitted, "And the draw to be with your mate heightens our sex drives."

"R-Really?" Aaron moaned again as he bucked into Grimley's hold.

"Really," Grimley confirmed, lowering his head to lap over Aaron's nipple.

Aaron grabbed at Grimley's head but missed, latching onto his horns instead. White hot need slammed into him. He growled and groaned as he gave his mate's nub a hard suckle.

"Grim!" Aaron shouted, his back bowing.

Realizing what he did, Grimley eased off the nub as he released his mate's dick. He lifted his head and met Aaron's gaze. Then he carefully gripped Aaron's hands and pried them off of his horns.

"Please know, my mate," Grimley purred, seeing Aaron's confused expression. "I *love* you touching my horns, but I can't think when you do that."

"Th-That good?" Aaron's lips actually curved into a sly smile.

Grimley chuckled roughly. "Yes. *That good.*" Then he sobered as he skimmed his fingertips up Aaron's straining erection. "Do you want me to ride your dick, Aaron?" Upon seeing his mate's eyebrows shoot up, Grimley smirked. "Or perhaps you would like me on my knees so you can pound into my ass as hard as you can."

Aaron's lips parted on a gasp. His nostrils flared. He even swallowed so hard his Adam's apple bobbed.

"I-I—"

Then, somehow, Grimley managed to see a blush on Aaron's skin.

Aaron blew out a breath before saying, "I don't have any experience with this. Would it" —he paused a second, biting his bottom lip—"would it make me a bad lover if I wanted you to, um, ride me?" Then his voice lowered, and he admitted, "I don't know what to do, and I want to watch."

Grimley growled even as he grinned broadly. "Oh, my mate." He pecked a kiss to Aaron's lips. "That doesn't make you a bad lover at all."

As Grimley spoke, he used his tail to reach under a nearby pillow and grab the tube of lube he kept in the living space.

CHAPTER ELEVEN

Aaron licked his lips as he watched Grimley use his tail to draw out a tube of lube. His breathing hitched as the gargoyle used his thumb-claw to pop open the top before pouring some onto several inches at the tip of his tail. After Grimley closed it, he began moving his tail behind his body.

Then Grimley slung a leg over Aaron's waist while bracketing his head with his forearms. "You said you wanted to watch, but I don't think I can wait that long this time around," the gargoyle admitted, surprising Aaron. As Grimley skimmed the backs of his claws along Aaron's jawline, he whispered, "The way you touch me, my tail, my wings, my ears, my horns." He shuddered, his eyelids sliding to half-mast. "Everything sends my blood soaring with need."

Aaron could barely believe Grimley's words, but the gargoyle's hungry expression, the open need etched across his features, told the story as clearly as any comment ever could.

My touch is everything to this gargoyle.

Just . . . damn.

A wave of pride crashed over Aaron, followed by a healthy dose of humility.

I need to make certain I'm worthy of him.

"Stop thinking, Aaron," Grimley growled, pecking a kiss to his lips. "I want you any way I can get you."

Aaron realized his scent must have given away his sudden rise of nerves. The need to soothe Grimley rose within him, surprising him with its intensity. Still, he didn't fight it.

Lifting his arms, Aaron cradled Grimley's neck and massaged lightly. "Sometimes, the things you make me feel are overwhelming, Grim," he told him honestly. "But don't ever think I don't want this. I do. I truly do." Rubbing his palms down Grimley's hard, expansive torso, Aaron added, "Sometimes, it just takes my brain a minute or two to catch up with what my body already realizes."

"Oh?" Grimley teased his claws along Aaron's jaw. "And what does your body know?"

Scoffing, Aaron murmured, "That I'm yours."

As the words passed his lips, Aaron realized that no truer words had ever been uttered. He saw the smile of delight on Grimley's face, and while all those sharp teeth should have concerned him, instead, the expression excited him. Aaron had put that pleased, happy look on the big male, and something told him the gargoyle didn't smile nearly often enough.

Hell, the rusty sound when Grimley laughed was giveaway enough.

"Aaron." Grimley breathed his name as if it were a benediction. "My mate."

Then Grimley dipped his head and captured Aaron's lips. He thrust his tongue into his mouth, the long appendage caressing him. Grimley lapped and teased, ravishing Aaron with an abandon that Aaron hadn't ever experienced in his life.

Gripping Grimley's shoulders tightly, Aaron was happy to go along for the ride. Except, he didn't. Instead, he kissed back, licking and nipping, giving as good as he got.

Finally, when Aaron's lungs were screaming, he turned his head and sucked in a much-needed lungful of air. "Grimley," he whined, his need thrumming through him.

"I got you, Aaron," Grimley assured. "I'll take care of everything, my mate."

Before Aaron could tell Grimley that he wanted to know

how to take care of him, too, Grimley gripped his dick in a damp hand, telling him he'd added lube to his fingers at some point. Gasping upon feeling the gargoyle's calloused digits stroking his hard, sensitive length, Aaron lost his tongue and bucked into his lover's hold.

Gods, I have a new lover, and he's a gargoyle.

The thought flitted through Aaron's mind but drifted away swiftly enough. As right then, Grimley reared up to kneel over his hips. He spread his huge black wings behind him even as he peered at Aaron's groin.

Following Grimley's gaze, Aaron gasped, realizing he was lining himself up with his hole. He felt the pressure on his crown, and his jaw sagged open. His breath came in sharp pants, and when Grimley's body opened, wrapping his crown in tight heat, he groaned out his last breath.

As Aaron watched, Grimley sank onto his erection, taking him deeper and deeper. The heat and pressure swiftly went to his head, and Aaron groaned as his body instinctively bucked. He gasped with pleasure as he buried his erection into the sweetest chute he'd ever experienced.

"Grim!" Aaron shouted, shudders wracking him, but he couldn't hold still. "Oh, fuck. Grim!"

Aaron grabbed Grimley's thick thighs, using them as leverage. Then he planted his feet, bending his knees. Peering between them, he began jacking his hips, over and over, watching himself repeatedly disappear into the gargoyle's body.

Even as Aaron lost all ability to talk, he heard Grimley groan, the sound one of pure pleasure. The gargoyle's wings flapped, providing a slight breeze to Aaron's sweat-dampened flesh. His lover arched even as Aaron continued to pound into him, showcasing his long, thick erection.

Aaron couldn't stop his hips, his need to rut too great. Still, he found his attention snagged by Grimley's black dick. He managed to peel one hand away from his gargoyle's thigh and wrapped it around his lover's hard shaft.

Grimley roared and stiffened. His shaft pulsed and throbbed within his hold. In the next second, hot bursts of cum splattered over Aaron's body as Grimley came.

The feel of Grimley's chute muscles clenching went straight to Aaron's head . . . his little one. He drove himself deep as his balls pulled tight. Crying his gargoyle's name, he held on tight as his orgasm caused his senses to sing. His body arching, his neck flexing, he soaked his lover's channel.

Suddenly, Grimley draped over Aaron, flattening him to the hide beneath him. A second later, he felt his lover pressing kisses up his neck. Humming appreciatively, Aaron tipped his head to the side.

A second later, pain spiked through his shoulder. The fact that Grimley had bitten him registered, but a second later, the pain morphed into the most exquisite tingling pleasure he had ever experienced. The bliss traveled across his skin, through his veins, heating him inside and out.

When it reached Aaron's groin, he cried out in ecstasy, his orgasm blindsiding him.

Spots danced across his vision, even when Aaron tried to blink them back. As Grimley suckled at his neck, making his orgasm go on and on, he lost himself to the pleasure and floated away in bliss.

Aaron couldn't believe what a difference a week could make. As he lounged before the fire, naked as the day he was born and comfortable with it, he stretched his arms over his head. Turning his head, Aaron watched an equally naked Grimley fill a kettle in the kitchen.

Feeling a twinge in his rectum, Aaron smiled. The prior evening, he had finally gotten up the courage necessary to al-low Grimley to have his ass. He'd drank his gargoyle's blood and completed their bond.

Recalling Grimley going through molt—the process where Grimley morphed into his human form for the first time—Aaron felt distinctly relieved that no future changes would be painful. He'd liked the gargoyle's human form—big, broad, and dark-skinned, his lover had looked a lot like a body-builder—but he loved that Grimley had returned to his true form to make their breakfast. Aaron took a moment just to admire the sun reflecting off of Grimley's gorgeous, mottled black hide.

Smirking at him, Grimley sauntered across the room. He held the water carafe for their morning coffee in one hand while goods to make breakfast were stacked in the pan he would use was in his other hand. His gargoyle put a little extra swagger in his steps, making his half-hard prick swing invitingly.

Aaron felt his mouth water at the sight. Never in a million years would he have believed that he would enjoy sucking cock—well, he'd never actually given it any thought. Except, with Grimley's dick, he just couldn't seem to get enough of it.

Grimley chuckled, obviously having caught on to Aaron's thoughts. The way his gargoyle's black dick was beginning to thicken told him the same. Except, a few steps away from the fire, Grimley paused, tipped his head up, and narrowed his eyes.

A second later, Grimley sighed and turned to Aaron. "Get dressed, my mate. Someone approaches." As he spoke, he grabbed a loincloth from a small side table that was a new piece of furniture.

Considering Grimley's enhanced hearing, Aaron didn't bother to question him. He rose from their pile of blankets, hides, and pillows before the fire and hurried to the bedroom. While there was a bed in there, Aaron had yet to sleep in it. He loved their nest in the main room way too much.

After a quick wash and brushing of his teeth utilizing a

pitcher of water and basin on the nightstand, Aaron dried with a hand towel. He was pulling on his clothes, marveling at how easy it was for him to grow comfortable with the rustic accommodations, when he heard Chieftain Maelgwn's voice.

"Hello, the cabin," the chieftain called. "You guys up?"

"If we weren't before, we are now," Grimley responded loudly, his voice full of amusement. "Come on in. I'm making coffee."

"Ah, no thanks on the coffee," Maelgwn replied, although Aaron did hear the door open. "No offense, but I don't like your coffee."

Grimley snorted. "You're just spoiled with all that new-fangled shit."

"Could be." Maelgwn didn't sound at all abashed. "How's it going?"

"Check it out."

As Aaron exited the bedroom, fully dressed, he watched Grimley—a huge, proud-looking smile on his face—morph from his gargoyle form to his human one. His thick black muscled frame gleamed in the light of the fire, making Aaron's mouth water. His gargoyle had been holding his arms out to his sides, but as his body changed, he made a mad dash to grab his loincloth, keeping it from falling off his leaner hips.

Maelgwn let out a loud, bellowing cheer. Then he grabbed Grimley and gave him a hug. "Congratulations, my friend!" After thumping Grimley on the back, he rested his hands on his hips. Maelgwn spotted Aaron and gave him a wide smile as he stalked forward, arms wide. "Thank you for making one of my oldest friends complete."

Before Aaron could say anything, the gargoyle chieftain swept him into a firm, albeit gentle, hug. Even feeling a little disconcerted, he still returned the embrace.

Aaron quickly told him, "I'm really the lucky one. I feel so grateful." As Maelgwn released him, he added, "Grimley is an amazing man. Kind, gentle, patient." Smiling, Aaron focused on his lover. "Not to mention sexy as hell, regardless of what form he's in."

Chuckling deeply, Maelgwn patted Aaron lightly on the back. "That's just the kind of opinion I love to hear." Then he sobered as he watched Grimley hand Aaron a cup of coffee. "But that's not why I'm here."

Grimley didn't look surprised, and Aaron found himself leaning against him when his gargoyle—who'd returned to his true form once again—had wrapped his arm around his waist. "What's up, Chieftain?"

Maelgwn leaned against a prep counter. "Two things, actually," he told them. "Callahan Wistern is here."

"The vampire," Grimley commented, confirming Aaron's memory.

Aaron recalled Grimley telling him about Callahan coming to discreetly check Melanie's scent. He just wasn't certain how they intended to do that. Their plan became apparent a few seconds later.

"Also, over the last several days, Melanie has been loitering around town, visiting all her and Aaron's old haunts." Maelgwn grimaced as he curled his lip. "She's been spreading rumors about how he's run home after finding out she was pregnant and that he plans on skipping out on doing his duty to her and the child." Shaking his head, Maelgwn focused on Aaron. "I'm sorry, Aaron. If you want to have any peace or hope to run a business here, you'll need to make an appearance and help to clear this up."

"Aaron doesn't need to work," Grimley declared. "He can live here with me and never need another dime."

"True." Maelgwn lifted his hands, palms out in placation, even as he stared the larger gargoyle down. "But this is Aaron's reputation, so it's his choice on how he wants to play it." Meeting Aaron's gaze, he smiled. "Hell, we know the truth, and our contacts in town do, too. If you don't want to leave the estate for a decade, this wouldn't even be an issue." Shrugging, Maelgwn asked, "What would you like to do?"

Furrowing his brows, Aaron stared into his cup of coffee. While he would never say it to Grimley, he agreed with Maelgwn. He missed better coffee, but it was a small thing to give up in order to stay wrapped up in his lover's arms every night.

Still, that didn't mean Aaron wanted his name smeared by his ex—he'd even received the finished paperwork the prior day.

Maybe that was the catalyst that had pushed him to finally finish his bond with Grimley. He was finally free of Melanie. As it had turned out, her acceptance hadn't been required under certain circumstances.

Aaron had signed the house over to Melanie. He'd removed his name from their joint checking account, leaving her half, even though she didn't deserve it. He'd also closed their joint credit card accounts, and Chieftain Maelgwn had paid them off.

While Aaron had been damn embarrassed about that, the chieftain had assured Aaron that removing any leverage Melanie had over him, freeing him to be with a member of his clutch, was worth any price.

"Time to face Melanie," Aaron mused softly. Feeling Grimley's arm tense around his waist, hearing him growl, he peered up at his gargoyle. Cuddling tighter into his gargoyle, hugging him tight, Aaron told him, "I need to deal with this last hurdle, Grimley. I need to know."

Although, Aaron didn't hold out much hope. He hadn't been with Melanie for months before he'd discovered her cheating. That was the biggest reason he hadn't wanted to believe that she'd had more than one affair. While it wasn't often, they had still occasionally engaged in sex.

Maybe that was her keeping up appearances.

Pushing that thought away, knowing it would only depress him, Aaron forced a smile. "So, what's the plan?"

CHAPTER TWELVE

Grimley hadn't been in a human town, truly inside one, in over four hundred years. Back then, things had been oh-so-very different. While he'd sat in the trees and watched Durango being built, grow, and change over the last one hundred fifty years or so, he'd never freely walked the streets. True, Grimley had skulked in dark alleys every once in a while, curious about the humans settling in his area, but that had only been to gather enough information to keep his location a secret.

Sitting in a diner, at a table overlooking Main Street, was a completely new experience for Grimley, and that was saying something considering he was nearly a thousand years old.

"Try to relax," Aaron urged, rubbing his thigh discreetly under the table. "Your bouncing knee is giving away your nerves."

Grimley forced his leg to relax, but it wasn't easy. Only Aaron's wonderful scent was keeping him from taking off. Having molted only that morning, he felt as if he were being tossed into a pool when he couldn't swim.

Still, for his mate, Grimley would do anything, and there was no way he would allow his amazing human to be subjected to Melanie without him at his side.

"What can I get you, dearies?" An older woman stood at their table, a pad of paper in hand. She had a pen poised, ready to write, as she smiled at them. "Or do you have any questions?"

Grimley was a little disappointed that they weren't at

Goldy's Burgers and Bites. He'd heard fantastic things about Wren Cleaver's—Doc Perseus's human mate—restaurant.

Guess it's a good excuse to do this again.

Instead, they were at a different café, although Aziel and Jerome—who were seated across from them, and they'd already ordered—had assured him that the food was good. "Uh, how about your Denver omelet with the all-you-can-eat pancakes," Grimley requested.

The woman—her name tag read Dorothy—smiled widely at him. "Great choice, sugar." As she scribbled on her notepad, she turned her attention to Aaron. "What about you, sweetie?"

"Your full-sized biscuits and gravy meal, fried potatoes instead of hashbrowns, and a side of bacon, please," Aaron requested.

Dorothy hummed appreciatively. "Yum. Another excellent choice. I'll—"

"Ugh, you'll never lose weight eating all that. No wonder you're so fat." Melanie stalked to a stop beside their booth, resting her hands on her full hips. "Is this where all our money goes? Your stomach?" Realizing she'd drawn the focus of just about everyone, Melanie quickly morphed her expression into one of concern. "You know, you don't want to have a heart attack when our babe is still little. He or she will need you." Her wheedling voice immediately set Grimley's nerves on edge.

After a quick glance around, Grimley noticed from a few others' expressions that he wasn't the only one who wasn't impressed.

Pride flooded Grimley when, instead of rising to Melanie's bait, Aaron smiled at Dorothy and told her, "Thanks. That'll be all." As a concerned-looking Dorothy started moving slowly—very slowly—away, Aaron focused on Melanie. "Hello, Melanie. I already signed over my half of the house and the vehicle you drive. There's not much else I can do for you."

Grimley knew how difficult it was for Aaron to air his dirty laundry in front of everyone, but the clutch knew that Melanie had already done a fantastic job of it. At least, her version anyway.

"And what about our baby?" Melanie asked on a gasp. Her dark eyes were wide, and she touched a hand to her breasts in an exaggerated manner. "You would abandon us?"

Grimley glanced toward a booth off to the right where Callahan sat with Maelgwn, Tobias, and Einan. The vampire had his eyes narrowed, but he didn't make any indication either way about her truthfulness. Instead, the lithe blond male rose to his feet and headed her way.

Callahan bumped into Melanie's back, forcing her to take a step forward. Gripping her waist and upper arm, he smiled apologetically as he helped her straighten. "My apologies, ma'am." With a shrug, Callahan indicated to the right and a pair of pretty, young college ladies who were eating breakfast. "Got distracted by the scenery."

The women in question stared with wide eyes for a second, before they glanced between each other and resumed eating. That didn't stop them both from glancing discreetly at Callahan every few seconds. They even whispered a few words that Grimley's sensitive, paranormal hearing allowed him to make out—words about how handsome certain of Callahan's attributes were.

Melanie, however, narrowed her eyes and sneered. "Be more careful." At the same time, she wrenched her arm away from Callahan's grip.

While Callahan lifted his hands in placation, Grimley heard one of the pair of coeds mutter, "Bitch."

Grimley silently agreed.

Callahan continued on his way, pulling out his phone as he went.

Melanie turned back to face Aaron. "You and I have things to discuss," she declared, hands returning to her hips. "And since you keep running away from me and avoiding my calls, maybe we should do it right here." Melanie glanced around while snapping her fingers. "Chair for a pregnant lady, please."

A server down the aisle froze, staring at Melanie with wide eyes.

At the same time, Grimley's phone chimed. He quickly pulled it out and checked the text.

Not pregnant. She's just trying to manipulate him.

Discreetly, Grimley showed the message to Aaron. To his surprise, he saw the way his mate's shoulders sagged just a little. On top of that, he caught just the faintest whiff of his disappointment before he focused on Melanie again.

Even as Grimley wondered about that, the answer came swiftly enough. Aaron wanted to be a father. He recalled hearing about how Melanie had been the one to drag her feet, saying she wasn't ready.

Huh. I'll have to talk to my mate to find out if he's willing to carry a hatchling.

Something told Grimley that Aaron would say *yes*.

"Melanie, we both know you're not really pregnant," Aaron stated heavily. With a shake of his head, he continued, "I don't know what you think you're going to get out of this ruse, carrying on like this, but it won't work. We're done."

"We're not done until I say we're done," Melanie snapped. Then she cast a swift glance around and gave an exaggerated sniff. "And how can you say that? I have a positive pregnancy test. How dare you call me a liar."

Aaron frowned at her. "If you're willing to walk into a doctor's office with me and have them administer a test, then we'll talk. Even then"—his mate drew in a slow breath as his eyes narrowed, telling Grimley he was about to fight fire with fire—"how could I possibly trust that it was my child? I walked in on you with another man in our bed. Your physical trainer, remember? That's why I left you. What if it's his?" Folding his hands before him, Aaron continued, "I also know about the gifts you were receiving from the other men you were visiting. What if your babe is one of theirs?" Then Aaron narrowed his eyes as he leaned toward her. "Were you safe, Melanie? Did you get something and pass it on to me?"

With a gasp, Melanie swung.

Aaron tensed.

Grimley reached past Aaron and grabbed Melanie's wrist, stopping her from connecting.

"Let go of me," Melanie shrieked, and after a couple of seconds of glaring at her—where he fought his desire to crush her wrist for daring to lay a finger on his mate—Grimley released her.

"I suggest you leave, ma'am," a man stated. He wore a pair of black slacks and a pale blue polo shirt with a stain near the collar. "We don't appreciate flame wars here. This is a family restaurant." As Melanie gaped in what was probably feigned disbelief, the man—evidently the manager—turned his attention on their table. "The server will be bringing your meals in *to go* boxes along with the check."

Melanie curled her lip even as she spun on her heel. Casting a hate-filled glance over her shoulder, she stalked toward the entrance. A moment later, after one more angry look, Melanie disappeared out the door.

And that, folks, is what they mean by if looks could kill.

As they waited for their meals and the check, they exchanged glances.

Aziel's eyes were wide, but a smile teased around the corners of his lips. "Well, damn, bro." He leaned forward, resting his forearms on the table. "Never been kicked out of a restaurant before."

Even though Aziel finished with a wink, Grimley still scented Aaron's embarrassment.

Aaron managed to smirk as he responded gamely, "Well, you know me." He shrugged. "I always like to try new things."

While Jerome rolled his eyes, Aziel chuckled.

Dorothy arrived, and they sobered, taking their bags full of food boxes.

"I'm so sorry," Dorothy murmured, placing the check on the table, face down. The aging woman actually appeared pink as she glanced furtively over her shoulder before refocusing on them and whispering, "Kent is a newly hired manager, and I don't expect him to last long." She narrowed her eyes as she shook her head a smidge. "He just doesn't understand the meaning of tolerance, equality, or fair play." Sobering, Dorothy repeated, "My apologies. I hope you'll visit us again . . . after he's been let go." Those last words were muttered in a soft hiss.

"Not your fault," Jerome told her with a smile.

Aziel touched her forearm. "We understand that scenes are bad for business." He slid from the booth and rose. "It's a beautiful morning. We'll enjoy this at a table in the park. Did you include plasticware?"

Dorothy's eyes lit up. "Oh, let me get plenty for you." She smiled at Grimley. "And lots of extra syrup cups for the extra pancakes I included for your all-you-can-eat pancake request." With a wink, she added, "But I didn't charge you for that, since you obviously aren't going to be here to get all you can eat." Then Dorothy hurried away.

"I like her," Grimley rumbled, smiling as he wrapped an arm around Aaron's waist.

"Me, too." Jerome grabbed the ticket and headed toward the front. "I'll be sure she gets a big tip."

As they headed toward the front and the exit, Grimley overheard Einan ordering for their own meals to be put into *to go* boxes. He knew they would all follow along soon enough. Per Aziel's comment, they really would eat at the park. It truly was a lovely day, after all.

They piled into a large SUV owned by the estate, seeing as all four of them couldn't fit into Aziel's truck. Aaron's pick-up had been fixed, but it wasn't much larger. On top of that, Jerome had never bothered buying a vehicle. Chieftain Mael-gwn had plenty that those under his care could borrow.

Aziel drove, since he was the most knowledgeable about the town. Soon, they were pulling up beside a park. A couple of mothers were sitting on a bench, watching two youngsters race over play equipment, obviously enjoying a play date. Other than that, the area was quiet.

Piling from the SUV, Grimley grabbed two of the bags. Jerome snagged the third. The foursome headed toward a table in the sun near the edge of the forest. There was plenty of sunshine as well as a bit of solitude since they were on the other side of the park as the mothers and their children.

They quickly figured out the dishes and divvied up the food. When Dorothy said she'd been generous with the pancakes as well as the syrup, she hadn't been kidding. Grimley set aside his main dish and pulled the carton containing a stack of six massive, thick pancakes before him.

After sliding tabs of butter between each pancake, as well as a last one on top, Grimley poured tub after tub of syrup over the cakes. He'd nearly drowned them by the time he stopped, and there were several more plastic tubs of syrup on the table. As he picked up a plastic knife and fork, he heard Aaron moan with pleasure.

The noise went straight to Grimley's dick, drawing his attention. He grinned at his mate, who was happily enjoying his biscuits with rich sausage gravy. "Good?"

"So good," Aaron mumbled around his mouthful. He filled his fork with a large bite of fluffy biscuit, saturated in gravy, and stabbed a chunk of sausage. Then he held it up to Grimley's mouth. "Try it?"

Grimley hummed just at the scent. He opened his mouth quickly and took the offered food. As he chewed, he smiled and nodded.

Once Grimley had swallowed, he began cutting his own food. "Damn, that is damn delicious." As he stabbed a triangle stack of six pancake pieces, he asked, "Try mine?" Then Grimley shoved the bite into his own mouth.

As Aaron swallowed, he nodded.

After sliding his fork into three triangle pieces, Grimley offered them to Aaron. Watching his mate slip his fork into his mouth and take the food was a lesson in patience. His arousal surged, and he actually felt jealous of a damn piece of plastic.

Mentally rolling his eyes at himself, Grimley returned his attention to his pancakes.

"Ugh. I can't believe you're enabling his fat ass," Melanie snarled, her voice carrying over the park as she stalked toward him. She pinned a curled lip on Aaron. "You'll never lose weight that way, tubby."

"What the hell?" Aziel snarled, glaring at his ex-sister-in-law. "When did she start calling you that?"

"Huh." To Grimley's relief, Aaron didn't seem particularly upset. "That's a new one." He continued sliding his fork into his food. "What do you want now?"

"For you to come home," Melanie replied sweetly as she pulled a gun from her purse.

While Aaron and Aziel froze, Jerome muttered, "Oh good grief."

Grimley's attention remained fixed on the gun. "You're not going to shoot," he declared. As he spoke, he mentally calculated how much effort it would take to get his large body out of the small park bench.

"Well, I don't want to," Melanie replied, her smile looking

a little crazed. "But if you don't return with me and keep funding my lifestyle, Aaron, I don't really see a reason for you to keep living." Then her smile turned creepy. "And considering I know how slow you are at updating paperwork, I'm certain you haven't changed your life insurance policy yet." To Grimley's surprise, a tear actually trickled from the corner of Melanie's eye as she simpered, "Oh, no, Officer! My husband is dead? That's so terrible. We were going to divorce, but we were still friends. I'll miss him so much!"

"God, you're a psycho," Grimley growled.

"You can die first," Melanie declared, swinging the gun to point at his chest.

Perfect.

Lunging upward, Grimley broke the bench seat. He would feel bad later, especially since it caused Aaron to pitch sideways—except, it also meant his mate was falling to the ground, out of the line of fire. He leaped toward Melanie, barely resisting the urge to take on his true form, seeing as he noticed the mothers were still on the other side of the park. Instead, he took the two bullets Melanie managed to fire into his human form.

Pain spiraled through his torso, but he'd been shot before. From their origins, he knew she wasn't a good shot, and he would be fine. Landing in front of her, Grimley gripped her wrist. That time, he didn't resist his desire to break her bones.

Melanie screamed as she dropped the gun. When he released her, she fell, too, curling into a fetal position. Grimley used a foot to kick away her gun.

A second later, Maelgwn was at Grimley's side as well as Detective Desoto. When he arched a brow in question, his chieftain shrugged and told him, "I called him when she showed up and started spouting shit."

"Huh."

"Are you okay?" his chieftain asked, even as the detective began reading the injured woman her rights.

Grimley glanced down at his chest, noticing the red blooms spreading across his chest and ruining his shirt. "I'm fine," he assured.

A second later, Aaron stood before him. His mate reached for him, but he seemed to hesitate, as if uncertain if he should touch him. "What do you mean, you're fine?"

The fear in Aaron's voice caused a mixture of warmth and worry all at the same time.

"You've been shot," Aaron cried.

"I'm fine," Grimley assured. When Aaron continued to stare at him in horror, he sighed. After a glance over his shoulder, he put his back to the mothers, who were being talked to by Callahan and Einan, and tore open his shirt. "I'm really, really fine."

Grimley watched as Aaron stared at his chest. He knew what he would see. The wounds in his chest were quickly knitting themselves together. Within seconds, his body had expelled the bullets onto the grass, to be collected by Tobias. Then the wounds closed.

Aaron snapped his attention back to his face, his eyes wide. "How?"

Grimley smiled. "Gargoyle secrets," he whispered as he leaned close to rest his forehead against Aaron's. "The older the gargoyle, the stronger the gargoyle. That's why the elders lead us. They're damn near indestructible."

"Damn," Aaron whispered.

Chuckling, Grimley nodded. "Yep. Damn." Then he straightened and accepted a new shirt from Maelgwn. "Thanks."

As Grimley changed, their chieftain stated, "For the official record, Melanie missed, her shots going wild."

"Perfect," Grimley rumbled, righting his new shirt. Then he wrapped his arm around Aaron's waist and tucked him close. After a peck on his still-shocked mate's temple, he turned them back to their food. "Let's finish . . . hmmm." He took in the destroyed wooden bench. "I sure hope I didn't get any wood chips in our food. It was fucking fantastic. I wanna finish it."

Grimley reveled in Aaron's laughter, even if it was a bit higher pitched than normal.

When we get home, I'll spend hours proving to my mate that I'm just fine, so is he, and we will be together . . . forever.

About the Author

Charlie started writing fantasy when she was eight, and after stumbling onto her first erotic romance at age nineteen, she realized her true calling. She now focuses on writing gay erotic romance, normally of the paranormal variety, with heroes of all kinds. With the help and support of her husband, Charlie finally fulfilled one of her life-long goals . . . move to acreage with her horses. You can often find her curled up with her laptop and a cup of tea or glass of wine, creating her next adventure. Charlie enjoys exploring the mountains of her new Oregon home on horseback, 4-wheeler, or motorcycle.

She can be reached at ch.richards2010@yahoo.com

Or visit her at www.charlie-richards.com.

When Aaron Boltson discovers his wife cheating on him, he thinks his life is over—romantically, anyway. He can't imagine trusting another that way. Even flings don't sound good. Licking his wounds do, though. After all, if a woman who's supposed to love him unconditionally can't stand to touch his fat body, how could anyone else?

Her words, sure, but Aaron can't seem to get them out of his mind.

Aaron reaches out to his younger brother, Aziel, needing to get away. Aziel immediately books him a room in Durango, near where he still lives, and welcomes him with open arms. After a few days of vegging and relaxing, Aaron opens his door to Melanie—his soon-to-be ex-wife—who begins begging for reconciliation. Shocked, Aaron is grateful for Aziel's intervention.

Aziel rushes Aaron to a barbeque at the estate where he lives, but a gathering with lots of strangers—even welcoming ones—who are all in lovey-dovey partnerships is a little hard to stomach. Aaron retreats to a gorgeous garden maze maintained at the estate. From there, he takes refuge in the forest. Becoming lost, Aaron stumbles across the most stunning fairy-tale cottage he's ever seen.

When a monster appears, Aaron would have forever denied fainting . . . except he wakes in a bedroom with Aziel by his side. His brother reminds him of stories told by their long-deceased mother . . . things he had never thought to be true, and gives the monster a name—Grimley. Days later, as Aaron's memories of the beast plague him, he wonders why thoughts of searching for the reclusive Grimley seem far more compelling than returning his wife's urgent phone calls? Even with Aziel's tales of love, devotion, and companionship whispering in his ear, Aaron wonders what on earth he would possibly do if he actually spotted the beast again . . . other than faint a second time?

Meshing with the Gargoyle
Copyright © 2022 Charlie Richards
ISBN: 978-1-4874-3698-8
Cover art by Angela Waters

Published by eXtasy Books Inc

Look for us online at:
www.eXtasybooks.com